DARKWALKER 1
HUNTING GROUNDS

Original Publication (2012):

Copyright © 2012 John Urbancik
Published by Evileye Books
Editorial Director: A.N. Ommus
Consulting Editor: Greg Kishbaugh

New Edition

Copyright © 2018 John Urbancik
Layout, Design by John Urbancik
Cover Art Copyright © 2018 Mery-et Lescher
October Crow Font by Chad Savage/SinisterFont.com
All rights reserved

ISBN: 0-9983882-5-4
ISBN-13: 978-0-9983882-5-0 (DarkFluidity)

DARKWALKER 1
HUNTING GROUNDS

JOHN URBANCIK

CHAPTER ONE

1.

Jack Harlow returned to the bar from the bathrooms and asked for another beer and a shot of Jack Daniels. It didn't bother him much anymore, the things he saw; a man could grow used to that. It was the smiles, the nods, the acknowledgements — and the winks.

He wasn't a hunter, and he was never their victim. He knew it, they knew it, the whole damned underground knew it. He chased the whiskey with half the beer and averted his gaze as the Asian vampire strode by. She ran her fingers across his back as she passed anyway.

Through the mirror behind the bar, he watched her sashay to the door, hug and kiss the bouncer, and return to the night.

That wasn't lipstick she'd left on the bouncer's neck.

Jack hated being noticed. This time, the whole thing had been accidental. His bladder had sent him back there, nothing else; he hadn't noticed the vampire until she was already feeding.

"Don't you just hate that," a gruff voice asked him. "Struts in here like she owns the place."

The man was as tall as Jack, broader and paler. He shook his head until the vampire was gone, then turned to Jack with a smile. "Why don't you let me buy you a drink?"

"I don't take drinks from the dead," Jack told him.

The ghost shrugged.

A woman stepped up to the bar, through the ghost as if he wasn't there, and ordered a drink. The spirit grinned. "Now, that's what I'm talking about. You know how long it's been since I've had a good piece of flesh?"

Sometimes, they talked to him. Jack hated that, too.

2.

All Jack really wanted was to be left alone. Ignored. Forgotten. Maybe find an average, normal, nine-to-five somewhere. Get a job, a regular paycheck, a wife and kids. He could do without the white picket fence — and he didn't need the kids, either.

The first time he saw a *thing* was the night of his seventeenth birthday. He, Marie, and a few friends were working through beer and cigarettes in the basement of an abandoned house. There were no rumors about the place being haunted; the owners had put it on the market and left for South Carolina during the summer.

So there they were, drinking and getting high, doing all the things teenagers were supposed to do, when the lantern flickered out. It was a cheap electric bulb with cheap batteries, so not a big surprise. Someone banged it a few times on the concrete floor. Someone laughed. Someone put their hands around Jack's shoulders and hugged him close.

When the lantern came on, Marie screamed — so did one of the guys. Someone cursed. The lantern fell and cracked, and the light died again, but not before Jack saw what they'd seen: the woman with her arm around him, who had slid very comfortably next to him and seemed ready to nibble his ear or kiss his neck or whisper, was translucent. He felt the weight of her arm, her cool skin; he saw bones through her flesh, teeth under her smile, a skull behind her eyes.

One girl fainted, the others ran, but Jack turned calmly to the unreal woman.

"Wasn't that just *grand?*" she said. She faded away; he couldn't see in the dark, but she became less substantial. In the moment before becoming smoke and memory, she kissed him softly on the side of the mouth.

He might have seen things before that without being aware of it; he might have noticed oddities in the shadows and heard
voices that spoke to no one else. He might have smelled deeper layers of death in the cemetery or sensed eyes when no one was around. But that moment — the ghost in the basement — brought awareness.

3.

"Not very talkative tonight, are you?" the ghost asked.

The ghost occupied the woman's space, as if they were joined. Jack said, quietly, "No."

"Somewhere more private, is that what you want?" the ghost asked. "I've got stories that'll blow your mind." He laughed.

The bar was relatively old for Orlando, the music loud, and dancers packed the floor. There was the constant smell of excessive cologne, stale beer and cigarettes — and a mustiness underneath it all. The walls were bare brick in some places, probably fifty or sixty years old — plenty of time for a dead man to lay down roots. Maybe he'd been shot in the backroom, a drug deal gone bad or a debt unpaid, or he'd overdosed, but more likely, he'd been innocent, a bystander caught by a situation as random as lightning. They tended to linger when death was unexpected.

"Listen, it's not every day someone comes along I can talk with as freely as you," the ghost said. "I mean, there's plenty of fine young meat here, girls that'll coo and cower till they're pale in the face. But you, you're rare."

Jack laughed a monosyllabic snort.

"A *watcher*, here in my bar," the ghost said. "That's not every day. Vampires...shit, I see one or two of them a week. Even demons." He lowered his voice, confiding. "I tend to stay away from them. Scare the hell out of me."

Jack tightened his fists. It wouldn't do any good; he couldn't *hit* a ghost. The girl smiled as she turned, sipping her fresh drink, and left.

"We all play our roles," the ghost said. "Do you even know what you are?"

"Annoyed," Jack suggested.

"More fundamentally," the ghost said. "You've got s*ight*, man. You see what we see — you can see *us*. All of us and everything."

Jack closed his eyes. "I've been keeping records."

"That's good," the ghost said. "You're a Watcher, right? You're supposed to watch."

"Watcher, eh?" Jack had never heard the title. The things he saw — spirits, witches, werewolves — rarely wanted to converse.

"It's your role. Like mine is to haunt. And I'll be damned if I don't enjoy it."

Jack narrowed his eyes. "Aren't you already damned?"

"Semantics," the ghost said. "Anyway, it's not true. Being a creature of the night doesn't make me evil."

The music shifted, the dance floor thinned, and a crowd formed at the bar. Jack slipped aside, toward the door, but the ghost persisted. "Tell me things. What's it like out there? What's it like to breathe? I haven't had air in...I...I don't even know how long."

Jack stopped and turned to the spirit. He seemed nervous, floating from foot to foot as if shifting weight, and his eyes glistened as if wet. "Life," Jack told him, barely above a whisper, "is a series of dark nights. I see people die. I count the variations. I take odd jobs for cash sometimes, but mostly steal it from corpses. They don't usually care. I *watch* — because you're right, it's a role. All the world's a stage, right?" The ghost gave a dim smile. "When night fades, I crawl into a bed just like every other damned thing that stalks the night, and I do it because I don't know any better. You want to know what life is like? You want to feel breath? Ask her." He meant the woman with the drink but it didn't matter. "I haven't got one."

Jack turned and went out.

4.

The air smelled of cinnamon and jasmine. A tarot reader had set up a table right outside the bar. Ribbons of silk weaved through her hair, which had been dyed a variety of blondes, pinks, and blues without order. She shuffled ragged cards. Her skin was flawless and pale. Bracelets jangled, necklaces dangled. Her dress spread around her feet, even seated, like a sunburst. She had a precise quality to her look, and a hardness to her eyes that was rare in street frauds. But a fraud, she most certainly was.

A young girl had given the woman twenty bucks, for which the seer promised riches, a husband, the fulfillment of various generic wishes.

A tall gentleman stood unnoticed to the seer's right. Black suit, beard, and cane. His head had been shaved.

Jack had seen many things over the years. He knew the seer was false because he'd recognize someone gifted. He knew the names of most things. He had counted eleven types of vampires, seventeen things called ghosts, and all manner of "mythical" creatures. So he recognized an *ash stalker*, even when he had no idea what it was.

The man looked briefly at Jack, locking eyes — he looked at everyone hanging outside the bar. A shiver — an honest, spine-spanning *shiver* — rippled down Jack's back.

Ignoring it, or at least pretending to, Jack folded his arms across his chest and leaned against the brick wall within a small crowd outside the bar. The seer was just finishing up with the girl: "A long and wondrous future."

The stalker tapped the street twice with his cane. It was a dark wood, perhaps mahogany, something with a red tinge to it.

The girl rose, dizzy with visions of diamonds and gold, slightly tipsy but not quite drunk. She stumbled with only her first step. Her smile, genuine as it was, masked a shallow sadness.

The stranger strode past Jack without a glance, wielding the cane with his perfectly manicured right hand. A sigil of some sort was tattooed in the nape of his neck.

The girl and her stalker turned down a side street.

Jack, of course, followed.

It was a stupid trait, he knew, and would someday get him killed. But, as the ghost had insisted, he was a watcher. He watched, and recorded what he saw on an old laptop. Meticulously compiled dates, times, places, even the ambience. Moon phases. Temperatures. As if this information might be useful somewhere. It wasn't just something to do, but a compulsion.

Washington Street was darker than Orange Avenue but still well lit, sparsely used but not empty, with a pizza place at the corner, a police station down the road, and a public parking lot across the street. The girl was halfway down one of the aisles, walking between cars into a thicker darkness, an unnatural mist she didn't seem to notice.

Jack glanced toward the police station; but if anyone watched the street, the mist obscured him. Only three people existed in the dark: girl, stalker, and watcher.

Oblivious, the girl pulled keys from her purse.

"You won't be needing those." The stalker had closed the distance between them and folded his left hand over hers. She startled, pulling away from him, but couldn't free her hand.

His voice was clipped, the accent too well disguised to be traced. Maybe British. Maybe Russian.

"I...I should be getting home," the girl said, looking down.

"You are home." Releasing her hand, he lifted her chin to force her to look up at him. She reminded Jack of Silver Screen starlets, black and white beauties long deceased. He wanted to help her, call out or somehow interfere. The stalker tapped the ground with his cane.

A flash of dark penetrated the mist, and the girl became ash. The man inhaled. She flowed into his nostrils like cocaine. He consumed her whole body with one inhalation, and leaned heavily on his cane as he did so.

Morbidly, Jack wished he could see the man's face.

The mist dissipated.

The man tapped his cane again, turned briskly on his heels, and strode in Jack's direction. The cane barely made a sound. He stopped next to Jack but didn't look at him. "I appreciate privacy."

"Of course," Jack said. He suppressed his anger, his frustration, his impatience. It had never done him any good.

"I don't like being watched."

"Nobody does."

The man tossed Jack a coin. "For your troubles."

As the stalker walked away, Jack examined the gift: a fresh 1926 ten dollar gold coin. Sighing, he pocketed the coin and fished out his own keys. He'd had enough interaction for one night.

5.

On a typical night, Jack only saw one, maybe two things worth noting, maybe only autonomous shadows or red-eyed rats. They rarely acknowledged him. Three times tonight: a wink, a conversation, and...what, a threat? And it was still an hour before midnight.

It was called the Witching Hour, and the air changed with the day. Ghosts became more vocal and visible. Some creatures emerged only after the twelfth strike of the clock. Others strictly occupied twilight. There was no single set of rules — except they generally ignored Jack. He'd never figured out why.

He'd wondered if he was meant to defend their chosen victims. He'd sharpened some stakes and bought a Bowie knife with a silver blade, but it felt wrong. There was no easy way to describe it. His first attempt to hunt, his Mustang refused to start. When he walked, it rained — not a light drizzle, but heavy, splattering drops. A black cat on a fence shook its head at him. People got in his way. His head ached. His stomach revolted. He retched for thirty minutes, giving up every scrap of bile in his gut, just for the idea.

When he'd turned around and given up, wind and rain ceased. The Mustang started without a hitch the next day.

Another time, he moved with sideways intent, strolling casually, unarmed, unprepared, unconcerned, waiting for something to strike his interest. He confronted a beast disguised as a man. The beast had a victim, a girl, whom it would have been content to feed from without killing; it cracked her neck and dropped her body at Jack's feet. It hissed. Jack was paralyzed, not by fear, but by invisible chains suddenly binding every limb and muscle. He struggled to move, but couldn't even retreat as the beast disguised as a man sniffed at him, and licked his cheek with a rough, inhuman tongue. The saliva burned. The beast pulled back sharply, raised its claws, and seemed very close to ripping Jack's insides out through his throat. It didn't. *It couldn't.* No more than Jack could do anything to stop it. After the beast finally left, Jack collapsed next to the dead girl and, silently and inside where it counted most, cried for her.

Some nights were clean, completely uneventful, and he managed seven hours of sleep.

No night had ever been like tonight. *Not even midnight yet.* A wink, a conversation, and a threat. Did it mean anything?

Probably not. A real seer might give him answers, but they rarely said anything useful. "You can see, yes, so watch." *Watch.* That's all he did. Jack walked in the dark, watching, not knowing why, unable to choose any other path.

Jack had left his car on Jefferson, away from the busy downtown area, between railroad tracks and the interstate. As he neared it, there was movement in the shadows.

This was neither supernatural nor inexplicable. Teenagers. Knife-wielding, attitude-wearing, drugged-up little shits who had been getting high behind the fence when they saw Jack walking alone and thought it'd be a good idea to hit him up for cash . Beat him, kill him, whatever it took. Young. Stupid.

A useless fence ended abruptly at the edge of the parking lot; anyone could walk around it. Jack was already on the far side, away from the police station, downtown, and most street lamps.

The moon, waxing and nearly full, cast plenty of light. Despite the heat, the "leader" of this pack wore a leather jacket. He tossed a pathetic switchblade from hand to hand.

Jack rolled his eyes.

"M-m-maybe this isn't such a good idea," one of two followers said, blinking excessively and rubbing his palms down the sides of his jeans. It wasn't meant for Jack to hear.

Jack did not step away. Only the leader seemed fully intent on scoring this fight; the others trailed behind him, perhaps sensing the same thing that prevented vampires from drinking Jack's blood.

"Yeah, I figure you got a wad of cash in them pockets, bro, and I figure you're gonna just hand it over nice and friendly like, ain't that right?" A pale scar streaked the side of his face, from the corner of his eye to his ear.

Jack showed his empty palms. "Don't want trouble."

"Too late, ain't that right, boys?" He glanced to his left and right, but had to look all the way behind him to see his *posse* fleeing from the strangeness, the danger Jack exuded, the slight tint of dark he'd absorbed. It made him unpalatable even to mundane threats.

They ran. "Fuckin' wimps," the leader said, turning back to Jack.

"You don't want me," Jack said.

"And why the fuck not?"

"Got nothing for you," Jack said. He hadn't reached for a weapon, never puffed himself up. He *could* fight, if necessary. But maybe he counted on that mark, that ability to walk through seemingly anything. He didn't consider this kid a real threat. It wasn't like they were an actual gang. A pack of kids with more guts than brains, yes, and perhaps chemicals mixed with the blood in their veins. But dangerous? Compared to the stalker with the shaved head and cane? Not a chance.

"Aw, shit," the guy said, finally turning and chasing after his friends.

6.

Jack Harlow didn't officially became owner of the '69 Mustang until his mother's death, though he'd rebuilt the engine before that. The blue was faded, but there wasn't a spot of rust. Mach I 428 CJ Fastback. Scoop on the hood. It looked mean when its four headlights stared you down. The only drawback was the automatic transmission.

Everything Jack owned was in the car: a bag of clothes and the laptop.

He spent some time recording tonight's encounters, omitting the kids at the parking lot, then slid the laptop back under his seat. The Mustang roared to life when he turned the key. Lights blazed. It was a five-minute drive to the thirty-dollar motel where he'd bought three nights. This was the third.

He hadn't decided to leave, but hadn't yet bought another night. Thirty bucks was thirty bucks, especially when all your jobs were cash at the end of the day. He hadn't worked in almost two weeks. That whole *stealing from the dead* he'd told the ghost — that was rare. Like the ashed girl in the parking lot, victims usually took their money when they vanished without a trace.

7.

The room was typical of cheap motels: springy bed, mold in the corners of the shower stall, a 20-inch television that got HBO and ESPN. Pale beige carpeting, heavy brown drapes, a musty odor that outright refused to be vanquished despite three scented candles.

He usually slept dreamlessly, only sometimes in his car, but rarely went to bed before four.

Midnight passed without incident.

Half an hour later, still trying to get comfortable, Jack heard voices outside his room.

Jack Harlow had heard a lot of voices. They didn't always belong to people, living or dead. Many spoke randomly. "The Devil made me do it" could often be blamed on mental instability or outright insanity, but sometimes there *were* voices saying "Kill your neighbor's dog" or "Get the butcher's knife from the kitchen" or "Blue pizza pitch delight."

Jack didn't trust voices. He didn't listen to them. He sure as hell didn't question them.

These particular voices belonged to regular, everyday people stumbling to their motel room, two distinct males, one female. Their whispers carried weight, pushing through the walls. The words were unimportant.

But they echoed in a way words weren't supposed to echo, as if caught within a bubble. They bounced back and forth, doubling and trebling and folding over themselves.

Red numbers on the clock: 12:38. Jack rolled over to look at the ghost sitting on the side of his bed.

"Thought you were asleep," she said.

"Not that lucky."

She was barely visible, a wisp in the air, facing away from Jack. She leaned forward, as if about to push herself to her feet. "And I can't really scare you any, can I? Not like a regular person."

"Guess not."

"Do you know the way out? To the light, I mean. I hear about it, and I'm told I should go there, but I can't see it. I can't see anything. I always thought, when I died, I'd be able to see again." She paused. "Can't."

"Don't know," Jack said. "Maybe it's warm?"

"You're warm," she said. "But I see what you mean. Well, not really *see*." She forced a little laugh.

She sounded young. No notes of sadness or desperation tinged her voice, just acceptance. Jack felt sorry for her. "You died here?"

"In this very bed."

Jack sighed, and unconsciously shifted.

"It didn't hurt," she said. "Not really. It was just a little...surprising."

"I can't help you," Jack told her.

The voices outside were gone. Now, silence echoed within the ghost. "I'll go into the warmth. Like you said." Then she faded into nothingness.

CHAPTER TWO

1.

By day, Lisa Sparrow worked in an office in Winter Park. Her window gave her an obscured view of the interstate. It was a good job that never came home and paid well. By taking lunch late, the second half of her work day was almost over before it began. She sat at a computer most of the day editing massive reports before they were delivered to clients. They gave her time off when she needed it. She was never alone in the office, but could play music at her desk with the volume low. Though she had an actual office, not a cubicle, half that space doubled as the copy room.

It was thoroughly unfulfilling.

Her small downtown apartment was high rent but affordable. Her car was a few years old; she planned to keep it until she saved enough to upgrade to a Mercedes. The paintings on her walls were real oils on canvases done by local artists. She didn't see the point in prints. Picasso on the wall only reminded her she'd never afford the original.

Her bedroom was barely large enough for her king-sized bed. The kitchen, dining room, and living room were a single open space big enough for two people. She never threw parties.

Lisa kept a dream journal by her bed. It contained fields of flowers, rainbows, horses — typical, non-nightmarish things. When she dreamt of the dark, she was surrounded by cats and owls, friends and lovers. The moon was always bright. The lights never failed. When her dreams turned sexual, her partner was always the same anonymous stranger. She wished she had those dreams more often. Other dreams were — difficult to describe.

Nightmares sometimes woke her. She'd turn on the light, get a drink of water, look at the clock, and wonder why in hell she was up at 5AM. This was one of those mornings. The time was 4:47.

Lisa Sparrow yawned and filled a glass from the tap. She'd been out dancing. If she believed every guy who ever tried to get in her pants, she was beautiful. Before dawn, without make-up, her hair askew, she didn't care.

She rinsed her face, swallowed two gulps of water, and looked out the window.

It was like a painting. The window was almost as big as the wall; three panes, separated by thin black strips looked down on Lake Eola. From the fifth floor, she saw trees, other buildings, but no streets. It was as much landscape as cityscape, which allowed her to forget the troubles of the world — and the her vague, unremembered nightmares.

She was awake. There was no going back to bed, not for just another sixty minutes. She started the coffee machine, and stretched on the hardwood floor, toe touches and the like. She worked her arms and neck, did a few dozen crunches, then changed into jogging clothes.

The path around the lake was almost one mile exactly. She circled it four times before going back to shower for work. She'd pay for the lack of sleep later, but she could always get to bed early tonight.

At least, that's how she planned it.

2.

At 5:30 in the morning, well before sunrise, Jack Harlow slept. It would be his last night in the seedy motel. The ghost of a girl fluttered nearby, unable to see him but comforted by his warmth.

3.

Frank Thompson, delivering newspapers to drugstores and supermarkets, paused briefly to glance at the clock on his dashboard. His unshaven face itched. The truck smelled of news ink.

His route was the same every morning, seven days a week. He started at four and got home by ten — plenty of time to watch games, bet horses, or toss a ball with nine-year-old Frankie Junior.

He hauled a bundle of papers out of the back of the truck and lugged it to the card shop. Since the supermarket next door had shut down, this corner of the shopping center was dark. The shop wouldn't open for hours.

Frank Thompson wouldn't live to see dawn.

The thing waiting in the shadows was small, skinny, unthreatening — but fast. Its razor claws slashed paper and clothing and flesh, catching only on the bones.

Frank was strong enough a man to push the thing off him. Once. It rolled on the ground like a ball, then popped back, claws extended and teeth bared. Those yellow, feral eyes were the last thing Frank saw.

4.

Jack Harlow spent the morning moving lumber. It was day labor, a few hours and enough money for another night at the motel.

He earned a good deal of sweat and got his blood pumping. He always felt reinvigorated after doing physical work. This type of job was a workout that cleared his mind.

Long ago, he'd ceased feeling horror. The death of innocents didn't affect him like it used to. The first time he saw blood, he'd vomited and shook and nearly passed out. He still felt pity. Compassion. But he'd learned to rationalize that there was no such thing as innocent: the slaughtered waitress might have been skimming cash from the till, the devoured stock broker probably cheated on his wife.

He rarely saw death. Most creatures, after taking what they needed, left their victims disoriented but very much alive. If not most, many. Some. Rarely in front of Jack.

The thing in the parking lot last night, however, had burnt that girl to ash so quickly there'd been no time for pain. She might have even felt safe, locked in his eyes. Maybe, for her, death was a release. Maybe.

Physical exhaustion was a blessing. When the body shut down, the mind followed. No rattling of chains or echoing voices would stir him. He could sleep the whole night through.

5.

Lisa Sparrow's day at work was typical. The printer broke while most of the office was out to lunch, giving her a fifteen-minute respite. She'd brought lunch and ate in the break room while reading the newspaper.

She didn't really read the newspaper. She checked the funnies, which were never as funny as she remembered, and worked the crossword. Usually, she solved all but a few scattered letters.

Today, she finished it with time to spare.

The phone rang a few minutes before quitting time. "Come out and play tonight."

Liz always kept Lisa out until all hours of the night seeking new bars, new clubs, new experiences. "There's a band tonight at The Precipice."

"*The Precipice*? Have we ever been there?"

"*We* haven't, no," Liz said. "But I have. You'll love it. It'll love you. It's better than wasting time in those other places. And it's ladies night. Free drinks. I'll pick you up at ten."

Lisa was already tired.

CHAPTER THREE

1.

Nick Hunter wasn't born with that name. Hunter was as much vocation. He hunted at night.

His pick-up was loaded with a variety of weapons and tools. He'd trained for years in hand to hand combat. Knew how to use a staff, a sword, a bow, and a gun. The scar next to his left eye so slight, you had to know it was there to see it; another on his arm was plainly visible, a straight red slash from shoulder to elbow. The first, he got as a child falling off a fence. The latter had been made by a vampire's desperate last gasp.

He'd had a partner once, but lost her to the other side. He'd pinned her to the earth with a stake and cut off her head. It was ugly work, and it paid shit, but it was a calling. A mission. A divine mission, one might say. Nick would, except he believed in neither God nor gods. He held his fate firmly in his own grasp. He lived and killed by the sword.

He didn't hunt for fun or sport, but out of obligation. He'd survived a cemetery slaughter when he was thirteen.

Graves were supposed to be final resting places. Consecrated earth. Holy. Sacred. They were not supposed to be cesspools from which Hell's spawn erupted. Three creatures swept through his friends, his sister and brother, spraying blood everywhere.

One of the creatures had ripped his sister open, reached into her body up to its elbows to pull out muscles, organs, and bones.

Thirteen years old, Nick fled. One of his friends ran alongside him. Nick had always been fast. The creature caught his friend first.

The cemetery wasn't far from home. He left a trail of bloody footprints to his house, shut and locked the door, and screamed for mom or dad. Both were home. The creature tore the door from its frame. Only the one had followed him, but it was enough; half an instant later, his parents were dead.

The shotgun echoed like thunder. Nick's hearing wouldn't be normal for days. The creature's chest burst open in a rain of gore. Nick clenched his eyes.

Chris Hunter had rescued him. Raised him. Trained him. And died six years later.

It was dangerous work, hunting. Nick had been doing it since the cemetery. Almost ten years now. He never bothered himself with whether he'd live to see tomorrow; he cared only about how many of those vile things he could take out with him. It was dangerous, but he enjoyed it. After all, they'd robbed him of his childhood.

2.

Over time, a hunter developed a nose. Nick had slain three distinct kinds of vampire, but the basic elements never varied. They gave off a particular odor, a cross between blood and ash that lingered. He could almost track them to their lairs by scent alone.

Orlando, like any other city, had an infestation.

3.

It wasn't quite dusk when Nick Hunter parked downtown. He preferred small towns, where there might not be a lot of people, but that wasn't going to happen here. In bigger cities, there were a thousand little holes and alleys in which a creature might hide. Orlando wasn't quite a big city; it had a few square blocks of tall buildings, mainly banks, with some alleys and lanes between them. Mostly, it was a suburb of itself. It spread out, not up, and left plenty of space for trees, greenery of all kinds, even woods, and a scattering of small lakes. Miles separated downtown from Disney World.

Nick smelled them here, downtown, and he wasn't about to leave them to their business.

In either side of his jacket, he hid a half dozen stakes, both silver and wood. He kept a pistol holstered behind his back. Knife in his jacket, another at his ankle.

He cracked his knuckles and his neck, then set off.

He had parked between the interstate and the railroad. He had one thing in common with the beasts he hunted: a preference for the infrequent streets and alleys where they were less likely to be interrupted.

A series of warehouses ran alongside the tracks, parking lots isolating most. A fence surrounded one lot occupied only by a trailer-sized mobile office. Another building was square, red bricks with tiny windows.

Nick passed all this. Vampires made dens in the places where the buildings were tight. More places to hide. Closer quarters. Less chance of stray eyes.

In Nick's experience, they never slept in coffins.

The sun eased below the horizon as Nick reached an alley alongside an abandoned warehouse. Someone or something had claimed it as home. He could smell them.

Debris littered the alley; rusted metal frames, mostly unrecognizable, and random sheets of cut and bent metal. Besides the green Dumpster, the alley offered hiding places.

The garbage reeked of rotten food and chemicals. Rusted edges. One corner had rotted through. Roaches skittered about the ground there, in and out, oblivious to Nick's arrival.

Only the wind made any sound, a low whistle between the buildings.

The Dumpster lid squeaked when Nick opened it. He didn't expect to find anything, but had to be certain. The putrid odor struck him like a sucker punch. Thick black bags filled the bin. A few had broken open, spilling slimy foodstuffs that hadn't originally been black.

Nick lowered the lid slowly, then turned his attention to the abandoned warehouse. Someone had smashed three windows on the first floor, another two on the second. The top level was dark.

Their foul stench cut even the stink of the garbage. There were creatures insider here. More than one.

4.

Sometimes, the hunt was easy.

More than once, Nick Hunter walked into the nest, found the vampire asleep or groggy, and put a stake through its heart. Or sliced off its head in a single, uncontested stroke.

The worst? Tough to say. Could've been stalking Diane. Beyond ugly, it was tough. He'd considered quitting rather than hunting his lover, but when the time came, he drove a stake between her breasts. Squeezed his eyes shut as he chopped off her head.

No, it was the night he'd become an orphan.

Chris Hunter had been a hero, the ultimate father figure, just shy of a god. He'd taught Nick everything: how to fight, how to eat, how to speak properly. Related histories of the creatures they hunted, how they'd come from Europe on some of the earliest boats, wiped out Roanoke Colony and then the natives. He knew of at least a dozen different kinds, and was fairly confident three of those had been hunted to extinction.

They'd gone into a den at the crack of dawn. Eight beasts already asleep, another snarling at the intruders. They'd never found such a large conglomeration. Chris Hunter blasted the first creature's head off with a single shot. The hunters cut down the rest as they rose, wiping grins and startled looks from vampire faces. Fresh blood still stained their lips.

Two minutes, nine dead. Not a bad night on the job. Until a tenth came in from behind, twisted Chris Hunter's neck, and snapped his spine before they knew it was there.

Chris Hunter crumpled to the ground without melodramatics. Straight, eyes rolling back, sword in one hand, shotgun still in the other. No sound. No cry. No curse or breath, not even a last request.

Nick emptied his gun in the creature, filling it with holes, slowing but not stopping it. This one was stronger than most, older, and enraged. It rushed Nick. Met his sword instead.

Nick had dropped the pistol to hold the sword with both hands. The creature ran itself through to the hilt, snarling and spitting, eyes aflame, teeth gleaming. Nick pulled aside as it lashed out, getting his arm gouged instead of his chest. They fell sideways together. The beast clawed at the sword as Nick pulled a stake from his jacket. He drove it through the creature's throat and another into its heart. Then he yanked his sword free and beheaded the damned thing.

It was the first time he'd cried since the night Chris Hunter had rescued him.

5.

Nick Hunter climbed through the broken window. It was more than large enough for a man — or a creature carrying its victim.

Damn them.

Flashlight in one hand, gun in the other, Nick scanned the room he'd entered. It was an office, empty except for one cheap aluminum desk and a tattered chair.

He shined the light under the desk, into the corners, across the edges of the ceiling. The creatures could be anywhere. Their stink hurt his nose.

The door out was ajar. Half flimsy wood, half plastic window that had been smashed so violently, only a few shards remained. Nick pushed through, sweeping the light in a quick arc.

This entire wall had been lined with offices, maybe five or six of them. The rest of the warehouse was empty space. The bare rafters left few places to hide. The three story tall ceiling was air conditioning ducts and metal beams. There were stacks of skeletal beds, unfinished mattresses and box springs. Piles of broken wood pallets were leaned against the walls. This warehouse supplied its own stakes.

Immediately above the offices, a grated metal gangway outside a second floor of offices. They didn't continue to the third floor; the space there was empty and open. That would be the nest.

Getting there would be difficult. The stairs might creak as he climbed, and they only went to the second level. A ladder near the far back, a series of metal rungs built in the wall, was the only way up.

Just to be certain, Nick checked every office on his way. Most were completely empty. In one, a stack of papers had been left on the desk. Where the doors weren't open, the windows had been smashed, providing sunlight during the day.

The stairs groaned under Nick's weight. He winced with every step.

The gun felt deceptively reassuring in his right hand. Designed to slow, not stop. On the ladder, he'd be vulnerable.

He hesitated. How many were there?

They might already be awake. For all the light that reached the third floor, it might have been midnight. He heard nothing.

The moment's pause passed quickly. He stuffed the end of the flashlight in his mouth, kept the gun in hand, and pulled himself up.

The rungs, though showing some rust, were solid.

He peeked over the edge but saw only the outline of the blacked out windows. He took a deep breath, then pulled himself up and over the top.

Nick rolled forward, swinging the flashlight beam first ahead of him and then to the right.

One of the beasts launched at him, misjudging Nick's leap and pouncing on his legs. Nick shot a hole in its ugly white head. It fell sideways, almost over the edge. Nick slammed a stake into its chest before it could react. A fountain of blood, black in the dark, spewed forth.

Two more. He shot one. The other ducked and rushed forward. Didn't help, since Nick was still on his knees. Two shots, one to each knee. Silver bullets might not kill them, but the beasts couldn't walk on broken legs.

He staked the second. The creature spit up a sticky black phlegm. Eyes bulged.

Nick put a stake through the back of the third.

He waited a moment, rose, and swept the flashlight beam from end to end, across the ceiling, through the rafters, along the edge. He watched the windows. Listened. He heard only the whimpering of three wounded beasts. Mindless. Bone white skin. Not a hair on their bodies. Faces distorted. Vicious teeth.

In Nick's vast experience, this was the most common vampire.

He withdrew the knife from his boot and proceeded to cut off their heads.

6.

Midnight. Witching Hour. Jack Harlow opened his eyes.

The sleep had done him good. Jack felt rested, alert, anxious to get out into the night. He sat up. "You're still here?" he asked the ghost. Sitting at the end of the bed, she hadn't made a sound; she still looked away, either ashamed or coy.

"You're warm," she said.

He showered. Ghosts, when they did appear, rarely concerned him. With few exceptions, spirits had little impact on the physical world. They affected the senses, primarily vision and sometimes touch — a chill in the air, a breeze, rarely anything more substantial.

He kept the water cold and the shower brief, then toweled dry. The ghost never moved from the bed; she neither wavered nor vanished.

She'd been a pretty girl, a teenager when she died. Blonde curls, eyes clenched shut. She wore a simple bathrobe, relatively modern; she hadn't been dead for centuries or even decades. Maybe only weeks.

"You're going out," the ghost said.

Jack nodded, then remembered she couldn't see that. "Yep."

"It's awfully late, isn't it?"

He glanced at the clock. "Quarter past midnight."

"Awfully late."

"Not by my standards." Fresh cash in his wallet, he went out.

Jack found a club around the corner from last night's bar, on Court Street: red letters on the blackened window called it *The Precipice*.

37

The lights were low. Smoke filled the air and shrouding the dance floor in a haze. The walls, painted black, were dotted with irregularly shaped mirrors. Booths ran along one wall. The dancers were in the back, under a chandelier of prisms; rainbows revolved around the room.

The bar was toward the front, U-shaped, attached to one wall and stretching half way toward the dance floor. Jack went straight to the bartender and bought a beer.

He never danced and rarely mingled. But the atmosphere drew him. As alive as he'd felt after a good four-hour nap, the throbbing bass line powered his heart and kept the blood moving. Kept him sane. Compulsion drove him to seek the underground, to walk so near to the darkness that he felt its breath. He believed himself immune to the things he saw.

Why should tonight be an exception?

Jack finished the beer too quickly. The bartender happily supplied another.

7.

Change came suddenly.

Sometimes the build-up might stretch decades or centuries. But one moment, it happened; one chapter closed, another began. Change required no lead-in. It came and went at will, perhaps randomly, perhaps by the design of some higher power.

There were few other constants in the world.

Like when a caterpillar emerges from its cocoon, a butterfly now, its metamorphosis complete — skin shed, legs lost, wings grown — change was irrevocable.

8.

While Liz danced, Lisa Sparrow checked herself in the mirror. The bathroom was small; she'd waited most of ten minutes to get into a stall. When she finally got to the sink, it only ran cold. She rinsed her hands, touched up her lipstick, and generally liked what she saw.

Of the music, only the thunderous beat reached the bathrooms. They weren't in the bar itself, but through a back door in a hallway shared with another club and a few shops.

The crowd was all black leather, silk, lace, and dye. It wasn't quite a gothic crowd, but close. The music was all 80s and mostly danceable.

The hall was nearly empty; no one lingered outside the clubs. The bouncer checked her wristband and let her back in. But something in The Precipice had changed.

She recognized this as surely as she knew the difference between night and day. The music was muted, the lights dimmed. Eyes were on her. From every shadow, every booth, every corner, someone watched, studied, evaluated her.

The paranoia came suddenly, without warning — and without precedent. She hadn't dreamt of this place or what might happen here.

She saw Liz on the dance floor, eyes closed, swaying in slow motion as if through honey, as if every graceful movement met resistance.

Reflections — off the prism chandelier, off beer bottles, off eyeglasses — blinded Lisa. Her heart raced to catch the frenetic music. She almost stumbled.

Then she saw him.

Clichés raced through her head: tall, dark, handsome. Steady, penetrating mocha eyes. He exuded warmth, confidence, unpretentiousness. He'd been scanning the dance floor — no, the whole bar — but when his eyes found Lisa, they stopped dead.

Her stomach dropped. Palms sweat. She bit the corner of her lower lip, something she never did.

He looked hard, rough around the edges, but not in an overbearingly masculine way. She sensed softness, almost felt it. He was muscular, but not because of a gym.

No one else mattered. She barely heard the music, didn't feel her feet on the floor. She had dreamt of him, of someone who looked and smelled and seemed just like him, and she'd dreamt of him often enough to be concerned — concerned and excited — excited and overwhelmed.

She met his gaze, met it and kept it without faltering, without hesitation, without a second thought.

CHAPTER FOUR

1.

Jack Harlow stared at the woman in the black dress. Short, auburn hair; eyes of jade — or brown, he couldn't be certain in the light. The dress suggested more than it revealed. Fit. Subtly curved. And absolutely devastating.

He could not tear his gaze away. All other thoughts vanished. The blood paused in his veins. His mouth dried. He lost the ability to speak, couldn't even put a solid thought together. There might have been a bar, a street — even a city beyond that, a whole world — but not then. That moment, the entire galaxy condensed to the five-foot, six-inches in front of him.

He opened his mouth, found no words, closed it again.

She was *perfect.*

There'd been women in the past, short relationships that were mostly physical, but he'd never been stricken before. Never felt protective. Jealous. Possessive.

They stared at each other for an impossibly long time. Ages ended. Cities and mountains crumbled to dust. The universe imploded to a single atom then exploded again. Time warped, catching Jack in slow motion. Trapped — spellbound — in a moment of pure, unadulterated bliss.

She broke free of the spell well enough to manage a single word. "Hi."

He smiled. Jack Harlow rarely smiled. "Hi."

"I'm Lisa."

"Jack."

"Hello, Jack." She smiled now, too, brilliantly and gorgeously. She lifted her arm slowly, to shake hands, to introduce each other the way thousands of strangers did every day and night.

A sense of nervous awe washed over him. Jack Harlow had never been nervous, and never awestruck, in all the length of his memory.

Eyes still locked, he accepted her hand. Soft but solid. And in his hand, right where it belonged. She also glanced at their grip. Neither let go. The cold where they'd touched would be unbearable.

When she looked up again, still smiling, not releasing his grip, Jack's breath caught in his throat. Her eyes flashed from brown to green with the movement.

2.

Nick Hunter had nailed three of the bastards tonight. Half an hour past midnight, he hadn't found any others. It was vaguely plausible there had only been the three, that they'd resided here long enough to leave their stench everywhere, but Nick doubted it.

The warehouse district had nothing else.

He sat on the edge of a roof, legs dangling, looking out over Orlando. Downtown stretched a few blocks east and south; the surrounding streets were more suburban in nature. He liked it. Cozy. Quiet. A good place to vacation, perhaps take a week off, see what real people were like.

He liked to dream.

He sometimes wondered if he hunted the wrong places. Patrolling the East Coast of the United States left them free to do what they liked in China and France. Did Italian vampires have free reign over Milan? He'd never been west of the Mississippi. Never any need. He killed as many beasts as he could find and never ran out.

Granted, some nights he found nothing: an abandoned nest, the grisly remains of victims, even a self-immolated vampire once. But he always found clues, hints, suggestions.

His was important work.

This was his turf.

This city sprawled in all directions. In Nick's experience, the creatures tended to gravitate toward urban areas. More meat. Less publicity. Unless the town was small and isolated enough to be completely controlled — he'd heard of that, but never seen it.

He scanned the streets, though from here he could make out no details.

Ultimately, hunger drove him from the warehouse and into downtown. The bars would begin closing soon, and the creatures would come out to feast.

Tonight, the streets were quiet. Friday, Saturday, they might get a little more crowded with police directing traffic at the corners, kids passing out bright flyers for clubs or concerts.

Finding pizza was easy. Cheap and greasy and decent.

Wandering the streets, however, bored him. He detected nothing, saw no telltale signs of activity, smelled none of their awful residue — at least, nothing recent. They'd been here, walking these streets, passing for human while feeding on blood. But everyone seemed normal. No pale faces, no elongated eyeteeth, no misshapen features.

He knew several types; while the ugly beasts he'd slain earlier were common, he would still recognize the kinds that passed as human.

Half way till dawn, after the streets had cleared of all but a few stragglers, the clubs had closed, and the barkeeps had gone home, Nick Hunter gave up on downtown and tried the residential neighborhoods.

There were a lot of houses out there, apartments and condos, parks and schoolyards, all-night diners and convenience stores. There was plenty of ground to cover. Too many crevices into which a beast might crawl.

3.

It hadn't taken long to leave the club.

Neither Jack nor Lisa had any real control. An urgency overcame them, a sense of *now or never*. As if fate had always meant for them to be together — as if they'd been designed as a single piece, split apart and dropped separately on earth — but now that they'd come together, their time would be short.

They both felt it. Neither could explain it, so they surrendered to it.

4.

Lisa never told Liz she was leaving. Never had the chance. Too many people, music too loud, lights too low — she simply had to get away.

They walked the five blocks to her place, talking the whole time. She couldn't remember specifics about their conversation, nor generalities. Jack Harlow — she remembered him.

Lisa woke briefly at dawn. Her sleep had been untroubled. Jack slept close to her, softly breathing, still covered with a sheen of sweat. The perfume of sex filled the room. She rolled over, phoned the office, and left a message saying she'd be out today and maybe Friday, too.

When she hung up, Jack kissed her shoulder.

There'd been no awkwardness. Each seemed to know, intuitively, how to please the other. They were relentless. And Lisa definitively and unquestionably, understood the difference between making love and fucking.

She didn't want it to end.

5.

Jack Harlow, for the first time in many, many years, thought about stopping.

He barely remembered the time before he'd started wandering. Parents. Sister. The house on Long Island. Friends, classmates. A car, a driveway, a lawn to mow and a dog to walk. Bowling Saturday mornings when he was twelve, parties when he was fifteen. Pals, girlfriends, partners in the petty, insignificant crimes of childhood. Working on the Mustang, putting it back together, repairing this piece, replacing that part. Then the highway. Open road beneath the wheels, wind in his hair. Sun behind him, along with the cities, the towns, the people he'd met. Friends? Not in years. The road was tarred with asphalt, but pockmarked by all the things that bumped the night.

Those *things* existed everywhere. There was no outrunning them, no escaping, no place where he could be free. He'd been chasing an idea that didn't exist, his own personal Eldorado. Maybe the poets and bards had been right; perfection existed. Here. Now. No matter what eyes may watch. No matter what hid in the shadows.

Jack Harlow had run long enough. Maybe unknowingly, he'd always been running *here*, to Lisa. *Lisa Sparrow*. Her very name refuted the darkness he'd always known.

Was it possible to stop? Trade the road for a home? The Mustang for a roof? He'd keep the car, but he was willing to surrender the dark, the *Sight*. Give it or throw it away, he didn't care. He didn't need it. What had it done but erase his roots?

Next time a ghost spoke to him, he could ignore it. A vampire winking? Turn back to the bar. Wouldn't happen, not anymore. He'd never really been part of that world; always, he'd been outside — just like all the rest of his life.

Jack Harlow believed, truly and with all his heart, he could simply stop — for the promise and hope of love.

6.

When they finally got out of bed, near noon, Lisa made pasta. Jack stared out the window, hands behind his naked back. From here, downtown appeared to be an oasis of concrete and glass encased in a forest, Lake Eola in the foreground.

"I didn't paint it," Lis said, "I just rent it."

The phone had rung three times; she'd ignored it each time, but had eventually checked the number. Liz, Liz again, and Unknown. Liz had left messages. Concern, probably. "Didn't see you leave last night." Or, "Saw you go off with that guy..." She'd listen later.

Lisa settled for studying Jack's back. Well-toned, not overly built, no scars or blemishes, not quite smooth but definitely not rough. It had felt good, like flexible marble under a layer of silk. But his shoulders were tense.

This was it, she thought. Confessional. He'll fish a wedding ring from his pants. Killed his last girlfriend. He was gay, or only in it for the night. Ready to push off already, hit the road, find another city by sunset and another woman's.

She believed none of it.

Perhaps he waited for her confession. Husband away on a conference. Jealous boyfriend who'd phoned three times already this morning.

The water was boiling; she emptied the pasta box.

"How often do you see the sunrise?" Jack asked.

"Almost every morning," she told him.

He chuckled; she didn't hear it, but saw it in a ripple down his back. "I mean, how often are you up late enough to see it?"

"Almost never."

He said, "I see it almost every night. My clock's wrong."

She didn't quite know what he meant; was this some bizarre method of saying she'd been one in a long line of lovers, that the instant attraction she'd felt had not been shared? Or was his confession darker than that, deeper, more unique?

Darker, whether for good or bad, fit. He was not typical in any way. Quiet, perhaps — that went with the tall, dark, handsome motif. Dangerous even, but not to her.

"It's not my choice," Jack said, "but I seem to be a night creature."

"If you were a vampire," she said, "the sunlight through the window would have vaporized you by now."

He turned, nodded. "Maybe. Depends on the type." He paused. "I think I want to become part of the day again. Walk in the real world for a change."

The sauce and pasta going nicely, Lisa went to Jack and snaked her arms across his waist from behind, rested her cheek next to his, and whispered, "What world are you walking now?"

"Dark," he said. Nothing else. Hitman? Assassin? Secret agent? Lisa was intrigued, not scared, though she knew she should be.

"There's something about you," Jack said, folding his hands over hers. "Something that makes me believe I still have choices."

"You always have choices."

"I've always chosen how to *react*, not how to act." He turned, kissed her lightly.

After a moment, Lisa asked, "So what are the options?"

"I could run," he said. "Keep my life the way it was."

"Can you really?"

He tilted his head, those eyes burning into her, and said, "No, not really."

7.

After lunch, they slept — for real. Despite Jack's assertion that he wanted to walk in the light again, his body still operated on that wrong clock. The same since his seventeenth birthday.

Lisa had told him something about herself, where she worked and where she'd grown up. But Jack had no work to speak of, and no friends, not even among the dead.

When he woke, the sun had dipped beneath the skyline. The visible, western sky was bright with short-lived pinks and purples. Even the clouds, still fluffy, were colored.

Lisa breathed easily beside him.

He didn't know how to step out of the dark. He'd walked it so long, it had insinuated into every pore, every muscle, every sense. Could he really work the same job for more than a week?

He never had. No bank account, no paychecks, no home address because he had no need for one. His license listed a Long Island home that wasn't his anymore.

Could he have those things? Would he know how to use them?

Even in the light of day's end, he saw nocturnal birds flying across the sky. Three whippoorwills, which shouldn't have been so close to the city? Maybe nighthawks. They didn't look like owls. They flew independent of each other, not in formation. He watched until they disappeared. Two went south, one west, foraging and feeding, living the lives they'd been given. Maybe Jack had a chance to have a life different than the one he'd known?

He rose to get a better look outside.

As the sun settled lower, the pink sky darkened to red, the purple to indigo. Clouds thickened. Colored lights illuminated the fountain at the center of the small lake. Streetlamps blazed. People walked in and out of pools of light, oblivious to the shadows.

Even from here, Jack saw them.

A phantom in the park, floating one way then another, ignoring and being ignored; a half-wolf dog straining to break free of its master's leash; bats in the trees; a young man who was neither young nor a man stalking the shadows.

Seeing all of this in the single moment after sunset, Jack realized he couldn't run from his life. No matter how right it seemed, staying with Lisa was not truly an option.

While she slept, he gathered his clothes.

CHAPTER FIVE

1.

A fifteen-minute walk brought Jack to his car. He started it and turned on the radio (Billy Idol's "Hot in the City"), but didn't go anywhere.

"I'm stupid," he said to no one.

Second guesses — third guesses? Cause and effect. Was the dark responsible for his life? Could he ever take control of it?

He took the keys out of the car and walked. Aimlessly. Goals, aspirations, intentions — Jack lacked these. He flowed with the dark's tide and tracked things no one else saw. He'd gone mad the night he'd turned seventeen. No other explanation sufficed. Did he really believe in all these things? Maybe someone had slipped something into his beer that night and sent him spiraling into a world of cracked hallucinations and paranoia. As if, in all the world, *he* had been given this *Sight.* Hubris, that's what it was: an infallible belief in his own importance. He'd never been important, and felt less so now.

Jack thought he wandered aimlessly, but when he looked up again, he'd returned to Lake Eola. A few people, couples and small groups, walked around him with barely a glance. He had become invisible like all the things of the night. The moon was maybe a day from being full. The stars were bright, where not hidden by swift clouds. It was almost the end of October. The dark would soon be busy.

And what did that mean to Jack Harlow? Continued pointless nights recording details even he wouldn't ever examine? No, the only purpose to his laptop was to give authorities the ammunition to commit him. A nice room, maybe padded, with white walls and no windows, three meals a day, doctors, and orderlies. Until the dark infiltrated the asylum and destroyed it, freeing him for more of the same. Repeat the cycle in and out of institutions until death — and then, would he become one of the phantoms he'd been watching?

Fate had forgotten him.

He looked up the side of Lisa's apartment building. She was on the fifth floor. If she had been looking down, she might see him.

"Stupid," he said again.

A nearby streetlamp flickered and went dark. It happened to him all the time. It was not a sign of anything, but it sent a wave of melancholy through him. Jack sat on a bench. He barely saw the lake, the colored lights on the fountain and the spray of water, the owl standing sentinel on the snack shack across the lake.

Full night had descended without him noticing.

It was too early for the crowds to descend on the bars. There were just regular people out for an after-work stroll, with their dogs or lovers, enjoying the brisk air and completely unaware of Jack and his world. He preferred that. He didn't need the curious glances of passersby, questions he couldn't answer, taunts, disdain, or pity.

He glanced toward the apartment building several times. Rectangular and unremarkable. Brick and glass. No balconies.

Across the lake, the owl took flight. It wove through the trees, slipped from view, and dove to snatch its prey.

It was not an omen.

It was not a sign.

Owls hunted. It meant nothing, except that the bird was hungry. The myth of its wisdom was just a myth. Night offered no sagacity, not even in its animals; nor did it offer any pattern. It was random and unimportant — the very characteristics that made up Jack's life.

2.

At dusk, Nick Hunter walked through downtown. Up one side of Orange Avenue, down the other, then every crossroad. He walked slowly, casually — just someone looking for the bar or restaurant where he was supposed to meet friends.

There were signs throughout the city, suggestions that something had been here recently, something more than just those three fiends.

He walked slowly, taking a good whiff at the door to every bar, club, restaurant, and shop. He checked alleys, abandoned storefronts, empty lots, and parking garages. Near midnight, having found nothing, Nick headed back toward that lake. A jogging path surrounded it. An amphitheater stood at one end, with a snack shack, bicycle racks, and ticket window. A scattering of trees separated the lake from the streets.

A fountain ran in the center of the lake. A smaller, unlit fountain marked one corner of the path. There was a park, with slides and swings, at the other. Few apartment buildings rose between the path and streets, but no houses or shops. There was a veranda and even a manufactured beachfront. He doubted anyone swam here. In the dark, the water looked oily black.

The undead reek was strongest near the southeast corner of the lake.

3.

After a few hours of sitting, the same thoughts running through his mind (*Stupid, stupid, stupid, I should have stayed, I could have stayed*), Jack Harlow finally abandoned his downward spiral and stood.

Standing itself wasn't much of a statement.

He strode toward Lisa's building. He couldn't remember the apartment number. Hadn't there been some sort of directory by the door for a person to buzz in? She might not let him in, but at least he'd make the effort.

The street was mostly empty. The vestibule was a long corridor, wide enough to drive through, with two sets of double glass doors. The telephone pad was to the right of the second pair. Elevators were visible inside under bright fluorescent lights. Jack hesitated before entering, turned around twice, then noticed a wine shop across the street.

Taking a deep breath, he crossed.

4.

Showered, dressed, glancing at the clock and not caring how soon midnight would come, Lisa Sparrow left her apartment. The hall was quieter than usual. The elevator took its time answering her call, then sank slowly.

She didn't know where she was going. Same place as the night before, probably. Maybe she'd find Liz. Maybe it had all been just another dream. Her damned dreams.

Her heels echoed on the tiled floor.

The movement didn't make her feel any better. She shoved the glass door open, stepped out into the cool night. Three steps from the second door, less than half the distance to the street, she heard a clattering of nails. Feet tapping across the ceiling. A lizard-like tongue clicking.

She looked up both walls but saw nothing.

She heard the sounds again, behind her this time. Still nothing.

Another sound: the snap of teeth.

Up again, and she saw it: maybe three feet long, it hung from the ceiling by sharp, sharp nails. Long, flat ears, like a wolf or a cat. Big yellow eyes. Teeth. Ugly, stained, rotten teeth. Jagged teeth.

It licked its lips.

Then it fell.

5.

The thing dropped from the ceiling. Jack Harlow, bottle in hand, saw it before he saw Lisa there. All his years in the dark, he'd never seen anything like it.

He had nearly crossed the street. Now, he ran calling Lisa's name.

The thing had claws. Teeth. It was on her, shredding and tearing. They tumbled to the ground. She couldn't shove the thing off. Jack raised the bottle, an Australian shiraz, and swung at its head.

He sent the thing flying.

It still clutched a fistful of Lisa's hair as it smacked the wall and dropped to the concrete floor.

Jack swung again, missing, shattering the bottle on the wall with a spray of red wine and glass. The creature scampered aside, giggling, eyes afire. "She's mine!" it hissed, scaling the wall and looking down at Jack. It grinned hideously and pointed. "You interfered!"

Jack lunged, but it was quicker. The creature dropped to the ground. Bouncing, it cackled, "You is in trouble!"

Jack brandished the broken bottle like a knife. "Try me," he said.

"Or me," another voice said. The stranger swung a blade down at the creature's head — but his warning had given the thing time to scurry aside. The weapon severed one of its hands.

The creature screamed. High-pitched. Ear-piercing. It bounded out of the vestibule and into the night. The knifeman chased it.

Jack dropped the broken bottle and ran to Lisa's side. She panted, eyes wide, scratches across her face, arms, and chest, tattered clothes. Teeth clenched in pain. She found Jack's eyes. "What..."

"I don't know," he said. "I don't." He held her gently, not sure how seriously it had hurt her.

"You okay?" she asked.

"Me? Don't worry about me. You. I think we need a hospital."

"No," she said. "No, I'm fine. Fine. I'll be fine. Take me upstairs. Just that. Take me back to my apartment, Jack. That's all I need."

She pushed off the ground. Jack steadied her as she stood. She didn't seem badly hurt. No chunks of flesh missing, no broken bones, no serious bleeding. Dizzy, perhaps in shock. She leaned on Jack to walk, and they went inside.

6.

Nick Hunter chased the beast. It was fast. Too damned fast, even running on three limbs.

It didn't share the reek of typical vampires. It was something he'd never seen before. If he hadn't rounded that corner when he did, the thing would have slaughtered the woman and her companion.

He'd stuffed the knife back in his sheath. He'd intended to take the thing's head clean off.

Its blood was black, thicker than oil and tinted red, but it left no trail. It smelled more animal than vampire. And it was gone.

Nick should've been able to track it. *Catch* it. If it usually ran on all fours, the missing hand should've hobbled it. He drew his gun.

It had raced around the side of the building, toward the lake, and veered through the trees. Nick followed to the street, but couldn't see where it had gone. There were houses, a small restaurant, a bed and breakfast, driveways disappearing behind the houses.

The thing might've scaled the trees.

No fresh blood on the street. No witnesses staring with hanging jaws to indicate direction. Nothing had been knocked over or broken. It had left no tracks on either the sidewalk or the cobblestone street.

Nick looked up and aimed everywhere. Nothing moved, not even wind. He felt stupid. Foolish. Inadequate.

It wasn't a vampire. He didn't know that for certain, but he felt it. Believed it. But it was more like a vampire than a common criminal, and certainly not human. What else could it be? Anything. Anything at all. Nick realized, with a sudden heaviness, that if vampires existed, so did other creatures — demons, werewolves, fairies — dark, twisted out of reality, scarred and vicious.

CHAPTER SIX

1.

Lisa Sparrow tried to push out the memory of teeth, but the only other thing she remembered was claws. When she closed her eyes, the thing dropped on her again and again. Only Jack's touch chased it away. It wasn't sexual. He'd gotten her into her tub, tended her wounds, washed and rinsed them, and bandaged the worst. She'd let him.

"You're okay," Jack said. Again. His voice comforted her. Had he been coming back? Had fate intervened, sending him at that very moment? She suspected it had been nothing more than luck.

And love, she wanted to add, but she wouldn't hear it. Not yet. Lisa hadn't said much since getting upstairs. She closed her eyes, clenched her fists, and let Jack wash her.

2.

She wasn't badly hurt. Most of the scratches were superficial. Jack Harlow found a first aid kit under her sink and antibiotic creams for the cuts.

It had gotten her back worst. Deeper, crisscrossing scratches. No bites. If Jack had been any later…

If he'd been earlier, he might have prevented the whole thing. The creature would've skipped Lisa, just as all night things always ignored Jack.

"You'll be okay," Jack said, not the first time.

After Lisa began to relax, Jack helped her out of the tub. He toweled her dry, led her back to the bed and tucked her in.

She didn't really need the help. She could walk fine and see straight. Totally coherent. The initial shock had worn off.

"You'll be okay," he said. It had become a mantra by now. "I need to get some things."

"Leaving again?"

"I won't be long," Jack said. "I need some things from my car. I won't be thirty minutes."

Lisa nodded. "You know what that thing was?"

How much should he tell her? How much could she handle — or accept? "I don't think so," he finally said, "but I want to be sure."

He'd recorded things in his computer for years, building a database that might, in fact, include a creature just like this one. That was why he had the laptop. Memory played tricks. Time warped it. He didn't trust himself to cross-reference every little detail in his *head*.

So he'd been tracking this information with a purpose, after all.

He kissed her cheek, then her lips. "Half an hour."

He took her keys and locked the door on his way out.

The hall was empty but for a few spots of blood. The downstairs hall, with its tiled floor and mass produced art, was just as clean. Outside the glass doors, blood stained the ground.

Not human blood — this was blacker, easily mistaken for oil or even water. The severed hand was gone.

The streets were quiet and nearly barren. A small breeze chilled his back.

He didn't want to leave Lisa again, but he didn't know what he was dealing with. If the claws carried poisons, Lisa might be dying. He doubted it; those had been designed to tear and rend. But if he'd seen one before, maybe he could...what, fight it? Destroy it? It was long gone, and the knifeman with it. It wouldn't come back.

He hadn't gone fifty feet when the nearest streetlamp flickered out. Twice in one night, as if he interfered with the flow of electricity.

His Mustang was on the opposite side of downtown, maybe ten blocks west and a few more north, but by the time he reached the far end of the lake, Jack heard footsteps. They echoed his, but imprecisely. Off to the right, toward Lake Eola and the path which circled it. He saw nothing and no one.

He quickened his pace.

Past the lake, a few stores faced the street: a locksmith, a bookshop, a restaurant with people eating outside.

The footsteps came from his left now. Across the two-lane street, there were houses and trees and plenty of places to hide. The echoes stopped when Jack stopped.

Maybe they were normal sounds, his own feet bouncing off curved metallic objects, or cars, or 200-year-old oaks. He didn't believe it.

He crossed Magnolia, a one-way, three-lane street, where trees gave way to downtown's buildings. A lot of cars were parked along here, and in a private lot at the corner. He passed the library, a parking garage, a few clubs, a tattoo parlor.

The echoes came from above.

He turned down Orange, the main thoroughfare of downtown, and passed a row of clubs. Pretty people in designer clothes lined the sidewalks, partitioned from the rest of the world by velvet ropes, let in one at a time by a muscle in a tuxedo. A crowd of Goths gathered near the bar where the vampire had winked at him. In the black-painted window, a shimmering ghost stared at him. He had tried to tell Jack stories the other night.

He watched Jack approach with an expression resembling sorrow.

"Back for my stories, I hope? A drink, perhaps?" The ghost squinted, as if trying to look at Jack more closely. "Ah, but you have changed."

Jack stopped alongside the window, lowered his voice so as not be overheard. "Shouldn't you be off haunting something?"

"Oh, I am, really," the ghost said. "But you can't fault a man for curiosity. Kill a man for it, certainly, that's been done. Oh, I could tell you stories."

"So I've heard." People walked behind him, most ignoring him entirely, some sparing a second look. Jack might be examining the band flyers posted on the window.

"You're in trouble, aren't you?" the ghost asked. "Someplace you haven't been before. I can tell. You're the opposite of what you were. Attracting rather than repelling."

"If you have something to tell me," Jack said, "something so important you came to the very edge of your...habitat." Jack tapped, once, on the window, "quit fucking around and tell me."

The ghost smiled. After a minute, he said, "Come back when you have time for a story." He faded backwards, into the club.

3.

Quiet: the room, the whole apartment, the entire world. Sitting at the edge of her bed, staring out the window, Lisa Sparrow felt the thickness of silence.

She couldn't see the street, just the lake and the path around it, buildings on the other side, even the theatre. Movement, too, of people and night birds, shadows and silhouettes — merely shapes, all of them.

She didn't feel the scratches on her face, back, and chest. They had burned at first, itched afterwards, but now she wouldn't know they were there if the window didn't reflect them — and it did a poor job of that. She, and the room behind her, looked ghostly. The glass also reflected recent memories: yellow eyes and teeth, dropping, slashing, slicing, laughing.

It would be easier to forget Jack.

Would he come back? Did he feel as strongly as she suspected — as strongly as she felt? What did she feel? Better to focus on Jack Harlow, wandering mystery man, than the champing teeth. He dream journal included variations of both.

Midnight approached. The beginning of tomorrow. *Sleep, perchance to dream,* Hamlet had said, *what dreams may come?* None good for Lisa Sparrow.

Though tired, her eyes refused to shut before Jack returned. If he didn't, she would never sleep again. That thing would haunt her dreams. It would be better to sit on the end of the bed and never lay down again, stare outside until the sun rose and fell and rose again, endlessly, infinitely, until the very idea of dreaming disintegrated.

Lisa inhaled deeply and held the breath. It wasn't like her to fold up or collapse. She released the air slowly, through her mouth, as if expelling anxieties and tension.

She could prepare better next time. She could get pepper spray — or a gun. Take karate lessons and pump iron and cast spells that burned three-foot-tall teeth-baring creatures to ash. Pay more attention to her dreams. Life was simpler when she only had to worry about random shootings and terrorism.

Jack was out there. He had her key. He'd be back. Next to him, she could sleep. Dream of flowers and sunshine and — no, not sunshine. Jack belonged to the dark. It was something she should have realized right from the beginning —something he'd never be able to change. That's why he'd left.

But then he'd come back.

4.

The street grew darker as Jack passed the parking lot and police station. No kids got in his way this time. Still, he cast furtive glances left, right, over his shoulder. He watched the distance ahead and the sky above.

Footsteps, no longer mere echoes, followed him. Or paced him. Alongside? Ahead? He saw nothing, not even the things that never hid from his eyes. No sign of movement except trees in the wind, litter on the streets, normal living people in the parking lot or at the pizza place.

He didn't like it.

Jack couldn't shake the sensation of eyes — in the leaves, the bricks, the clouds, the street. The ghost had been right: he'd changed. Did the world feel different because he'd found hope?

The footsteps seemed human enough, not that clattering creature from Lisa's apartment. Solid, they belonged to no ghost — at least, no kind of phantom he'd ever seen. Vampires were generally stealthier. Werewolves shouldn't be out yet; the moon wasn't quite full, and they didn't walk like men. That left endless possibilities. Jack liked none.

Most likely, it was an echo, his imagination, the weird acoustics of a city too warm for October. A low pressure system moving in, planning to drop rain. The strange configuration of satellites in the sky, the position of Venus, something in retrograde. The last vestiges of Jack's sanity.

None of those choices appealed to him, either.

5.

After hours of searching, Nick Hunter gave up. He returned to the building where he first saw the creature.

The hand was gone, but bloodstains remained.

He didn't quite know what to do. Expand his hunt? Forget it and move on? Wait for someone or something to return with answers?

By default, he waited. It was easier than continuing a pointless pursuit but less final than surrendering.

Nothing moved in the shadows. As night progressed, the wind strengthened, making finding a scent more difficult. If it rained — there were enough clouds up there — he'd lose all hope of finding any traces of it.

Nothing skulked around the lake. He scanned the entire length of the path. He watched the park, studied the veranda, even the water's surface. He saw an owl, a cat, the normal things that moved through the night. But he realized, after a while, all these things moved in a single direction.

Once he noticed it, he couldn't avoid it. Shadows, a stray dog, a homeless man in camouflage, a pretty teenage girl — all flowed in a singular direction: downtown.

Nick tried to accept it as coincidence. Couldn't.

6.

Jack reached his car without incident. The footsteps stopped when he opened the Mustang. He didn't plan to search his database out in the open. There were too many eyes, too many he couldn't see. The dark had turned.

After locking the Mustang, he scrutinized everything around him — every tree, every lamppost, every scrap of paper in the street — and listened to each sound until he knew its exact origin. Night had never before held secrets from Jack Harlow.

He hurried back toward the apartment.

He avoided the ghost in the club by taking a different street. Echoing footsteps followed again, two pairs now. Right and left. Forward and above.

Around the corner from a shoe store, a cat sat on a newspaper vending machine. It was perfect black. Its wide green eyes followed Jack as he approached and passed. It flicked its tail once.

Under the footsteps, Jack heard whispering — nothing definitive, nothing he could grasp.

CHAPTER SEVEN

1.

Without a sound, Jack Harlow turned. He scanned all he saw, but noticed nothing. The whispering quieted. He said, "Come out."

No response.

"I *can* see you. And hear you," Jack said. "You can't play your games with me."

Whispers may have been just the wind. Faces in the windows might be shadows reconfigured by his imaginings. Footsteps? Laughing? Down the street, a couple, arm in arm, stumbled in his direction: regular people, drunk and happy.

Jack walked on.

Bats flew overhead. He was near the eastern shore of Lake Eola. He noticed the eyes of a rat in the alleys.

Laughter again — the couple had crossed the street and entered a parking garage. Their sound died suddenly. Unnaturally.

He stopped at a traffic light. Cars streaked by. Did the drivers slow to look at him?

When the cars cleared, he crossed. A path led straight toward the lake; he followed it. A lonely howl sounded in the distance: the call of a wolf — even in the city.

"I'm scared," she whispered, brushstrokes against Jack's ears. A chill rose around him even as he recognized the voice: the blind ghost from the hotel. Ghosts were usually restricted to a particular place.

"What are you afraid of?" he asked.

"The voices," she said. "The feet. I hear many things. *Many.*"

He looked around, but the whispering had ceased. The footsteps were silent. "Weren't you going into the light?"

"Can't see light," she said. "You said I should go to the warmth." She paused. "You're warm." He   didn't see her — or anyone else. He didn't stop walking. "I didn't mean for you to follow me. Isn't there a next step for you, something beyond being stuck here?"

"I don't feel stuck," she said. "Not anymore."

"Have you been with me all this time?"

It was another voice that answered. "Not all this time, no." The knifeman, holding a gun now, stepped out of the shadows. Not as tall as Jack, close cut blond hair, eyes masked by shadow, he looked older than he was.

The ghost said nothing. If the chill was any indication, she swung behind Jack as he turned to face the hunter.

"I didn't think you'd seen me," the hunter said. He held the pistol loosely, not quite aimed at Jack. "I followed the wind."

"The wind?"

"Strange, huh? That's what I thought."

They were bathed by moonbeams; no streetlights near them seemed to be lit. Jack had seen hunters before. Usually, they never noticed him. There should've been more space between them.

A vampire hunter, Jack decided. Most had little imagination, no inkling of what else existed.

"Not just the wind," the hunter said.

Jack felt it, too, how the wind came at him from all directions. It wasn't strong.

"Cats, rats, birds," the hunter said.

The chill behind Jack — the ghost — tensed. She pressed tight against him like feathers.

"Even them," Nick said, nodding toward a homeless man a hundred yards up the path. He stood there, head tilted, between lampposts, flexing the fingers of one hand open then shut, open then shut.

Jack Harlow had seen hunters in action twice. The first time, in the backroom of a club near Atlanta, a vampire sunk his teeth into his prey's neck — not the sexual game the victim seemed to expect. The vampire drank messily. A hunter came from the other end of the hall, stake in one hand, sword in the other, and buried the stake in the vampire's back before it knew the hunter existed. The victim dropped to floor, exhausted and hurt but not dead. The hunter took the vampire's head with one clean slice. Then he did the same to the victim. Jack had retreated deeper into the shadows as the hunter dragged the bodies, one at a time, through the back door into an alley and set fire to both. The vampire flashed. He burned so quickly, it seemed like he'd been made of paper and ash, and all traces of it dissipated in the air. The victim — whom the hunter expected would become a vampire — burned more slowly, less cleanly and completely. Still, the hunter was satisfied.

The second time, it was a team of two women, one acting as bait. She strolled along the dark pier, fully aware of the eyes upon her. Three vampires descended on her. These were the misshapen, pale-faced, hairless creatures a la *Nosferatu*. While she defended herself (and *well*) with a long, wooden spike, her partner shot the creatures with a crossbow. The bolts lodged deep into their backs. The bait slit their throats with a machete.

It was never pretty, the business of hunting. Jack stared at the hunter who had found him and wondered if he suspected Jack was a vampire. The stake would've already found its mark.

"Don't trust him," the ghost's voice said in Jack's ear. "He's warm, too, but he's cold. So very cold."

"So," the hunter finally said. "What was that thing?"

Jack hesitated. He didn't know how to answer. He went with the truth. "I've never seen anything like it."

"I have," the hunter said. "But not exactly like it. This was different."

"Very."

The vagrant in the path had come closer. Jack had not seen him approach.

He wore three or four layers, despite the relative warmth, and carried a switchblade in his unmoving hand. A mad vacancy glimmered in his eyes.

"And what about that?" the hunter asked, nodding toward the vagrant. "Not what it appears?"

Slowly, Jack shook his head. "I don't think so."

2.

Nick Hunter watched the homeless man carefully. The man walked slowly, leaning slightly to the left. His face was sandpaper, unshaven for days but not uncontrolled, his eyes wild and unfocused. The switchblade hung uneasily between gloved fingers. His clothes, tattered and layered, made him appear twice his size. He didn't seem to notice Nick at all. His eyes focused on the man Nick had found, the destination of the wind — of everything — a man who seemed almost calm.

These were not vampires, neither of them. The wind's destination appeared entirely human. The vagrant, however, was something else. The unwashed odor, the dirt and the grime, hid something.

"What are you?" Nick asked. He didn't take his eyes off the vagrant, but wasn't speaking to him.

"Me? Just Jack. That's all I am."

"Just Jack, eh?"

The vagrant lunged forward, suddenly agile and fast, the blade springing out. He swung it upwards, like pitching a softball, and grabbed for Jack's shoulder with the other hand.

Jack jumped back and to the side, putting the vagrant between him and Nick, the lake immediately behind him.

"You," the vagrant said, pointing at Jack with the blade. "You!"

"Me, *what?*" Jack asked.

The bum shook his head — as if trying to shake a cat loose — then jabbed the knife in the air again. "*You!*"

Nick aimed his gun at the back of the vagrant's head. "I think that's enough," he said. Jack, whoever and whatever he was, had answers he wanted.

The vagrant didn't acknowledge Nick. "You," he whispered.

"What's he accusing you of?" Nick asked. He could easily adjust his aim and put the bullet between Jack's eyes.

"I've done nothing."

The vagrant raised the knife to swing down. One step. Two.

Nick shot him. The bullet cleanly struck the back of the head. The vagrant's forward motion continued. He swung the knife down at Jack.

Jack fell sideways, the weight of the vagrant throwing him but the knife missing its mark. The vagrant laughed and raised the knife again.

Nick stepped forward and, from behind, pressed his own blade against the bum's throat. Purplish blood welled up at the neck; more oozed from the gunshot wound. "I don't know what you are," Nick said, "but I'm willing to bet you need your head, so you'd better give me one damned good reason not to cut it off."

Jack pulled himself off the ground as the bum dropped the switchblade and held both hands, open, palms up, to the sides.

So close, however, Nick got a good whiff of the vagrant. Whiskey. Cigarettes. Mold. Rotten eggs. Shit. Death. The bum was dead...had been when Nick shot him.

"He can't answer you," Jack said. "I...I don't think his type have much by way of intelligence."

"Meat," it said, spinning suddenly and grabbing for Nick's head. Nick forced his knife through its throat and, with a good knee to the dead man's ribs, sent it and its head into the lake.

"I didn't recognize it," Jack said. "I mean, I don't always. I knew it was *something*. But when it got close enough, when I smelled it..."

"Rank," Nick said.

"But normally," Jack said, "they ignore me."

Nick narrowed his eyes. There was only one proper response to such a comment. "What?"

"You're a hunter," Jack said. "You hunt...vampires, I imagine." Nick said nothing, but tightened the grip on both his weapons. "I can't hunt. I tried. I thought I could do something, but I can't. I can only watch."

"You're telling me this...why?" Nick asked.

"Because tonight, I hit one of them," Jack said. "The thing at the apartment. And now this." He glanced over the edge of the lake, and then returned his laptop computer. "Zombie, I think. Well, a variation." He opened up his computer and turned it on. "I'll check. I know I've seen his type before."

"You'll check?" Curious, Nick stepped around to see the computer screen.

Jack called up a database, hit a few keys, scrolled down a few screens. Finally, he stopped, pointed at the screen, and said, "There. Last September. Three of them. *Errant Zombies*. They didn't know they were dead, they thought they were...tramps, apparently. One had dried blood on the side of his head. They didn't say much, didn't do much, just sat in an alley. It was 60 degrees that night, cloudy, no rain. One snatched a rat running too close, bit its head off and tossed the body aside. But most of the rats gave them plenty of room. Even the roaches ignored them." He scrolled down the screen to keep reading, summarizing what he found. "A teenager turned down that alley. Drunk. Stupid. A bad ass, too, wanting to start trouble." He paused a moment. "After bashing his head in, they scooped the brains from his head and feasted until they were done." Done, he looked at Nick, his eyebrows furrowed. "They didn't acknowledge me in the least."

"You...*watched* this?" Nick asked. His stomach churned.

"That's what I do, apparently," Jack said. "Like you're a hunter. It's not by choice."

Nick stepped back, disturbed, bewildered, unsure of what to make of this. He could kill Jack here, now. This was beyond mere voyeurism.

Jack closed the computer. "That thing earlier, that I stopped at the apartment," Jack said. "Did you kill it?"

"Didn't find it," Nick said. "What was it?"

"I have no idea."

3.

Jack stared a moment at the hunter. He'd said a lot, maybe more than he'd ever said at one time. A hunter was one of the few people who might listen to Jack and not suspect he'd escaped an asylum. Still, Jack didn't know what would happen next. It wouldn't take much effort for the hunter to put that knife through Jack's throat and kick his headless body into the lake.

"I'm Jack Harlow," he finally said.

"Nick Hunter," the other said. "You have a file on hunters in there?"

"Some," Jack said. "Not you."

"You'll add me after this, though, won't you?"

Jack shrugged. "That's what I do. Like the ghost said, it's my role."

"Ghost?"

"There's more to the dark than vampires," Jack said. He motioned toward the lake, where the errant zombie's body floated like any other dead man on the water.

"You watch," Nick said, wiping blood off his blade. "You never get involved, is that right?"

"Basically," Jack said.

"Then why tonight?" Nick asked. "You bashed that thing's head pretty good before it ran off. Didn't look much like watching to me."

Jack didn't have an answer. He knew perfectly well why he'd protected Lisa.

"*I know*," the blind ghost whispered — for Jack's ears only.

Nick sheathed his knife. He kept it inside his jacket, out of sight but easy to reach. He'd already hidden his gun away. "I think I get it," Nick said. "I mean, I understand. I'd have done the same thing. Maybe. What's her name?"

"Lisa."

"Pretty name," Nick said. "Good luck." He turned to go, hesitated, and said, "Doesn't explain you, though."

"Doesn't explain what?" Jack asked.

"Look around," Nick said. "You tell me."

In the trees, Jack saw eyes, yellow and green: owls, three of them, perched precariously on the farthest, thinnest limbs; a cat beneath one of the trees; another on the paved path. Shadows swarmed within themselves. A snake, wound around a branch of the tree, lifted its head to meet Jack's gaze.

"You're being watched," Nick said.

"It's never been like this."

"And I don't feel comfortable in your spotlight," Nick said. The hunter walked into those shadows, deeper and deeper until the darkness swallowed him.

4.

Jack Harlow had seen many things in his life, but he'd always felt invisible and safe. The hunter had said *spotlight*. It was exactly right. The world focused on Jack now. Why? How? For how long?

All Jack wanted was to get back to Lisa, make sure she was okay, kill that damned — *imp*, that's what it was.

Names often — not always — came to him. He didn't make up errant zombie — or lycanthrope or revenant. Sometimes, he knew things by reputation. Ghosts, vampires, and witches all had stories and legends and myths. Sometimes, Jack knew instinctively which stories had an inkling of truth — as if he'd done this in a past life.

Imp. That was all he knew. Popular culture had no silver bullets or holy water to deal with such creatures. They were unique to Jack's experience.

One of the owls launched into the air. It flew low over Jack's head before veering away from the lake.

He walked slowly. Carefully. He made sure every step was light, soft, in the grass, so his feet didn't tap the asphalt. Some of these shadows lived — or approximated living. They watched and listened, just as Jack did.

Something had changed, something fundamental. Was it the imp? The vampire? The ghost in the club? Or was it the ghost that followed him, even now, clinging to his warmth because she could not see "the light"?

"Are you still there?" he asked.

No immediate answer.

"I know you can't see me, but I'm still warm, aren't I?"

"You are."

"You sound young."

"I was."

"You can't stay with me."

"There is no place else," she pleaded.

"There are hundreds of places. Thousands. Millions. But you must leave me."

"Why?" She choked on the word, ready to cry.

"What do you hear around me?"

"Whispering," she said, lowering her voice. "Voices. Footsteps. Questions. I hear no words, just the tone."

"They've been with me since you came," he said.

"No," she said.

"They have," Jack insisted. "My life was — not ordinary, but simple. Always the same. Not since you."

"I didn't bring them," she said. "I'm not bringing them, am I? I can't be. They weren't there from the beginning. When I touched you in the hotel..."

"Touched?" Jack asked.

She ignored the interruption. "There was nothing then. No one. Everything pretended you weren't there. Moved aside, even. It was hard to stay with you then. Now...now, I don't want to go. I'm drawn to you."

"Why?"

"The snapping thing. The clicking thing."

"The imp," Jack said.

She shivered. Jack felt the vibration in the chill around him. "It was awful," she said. "I hated to be near it."

If she was right, if the imp had changed things —
Jack had done it to himself. He'd interrupted, protecting
Lisa. He'd made himself a target. Whatever immunity
he'd had, he surrendered it the moment he interfered.

CHAPTER EIGHT

1.

Clouds gathered. They veiled the moon and threatened. The weatherman had said they'd come, and that early Friday they'd bring rain. But the moon still shone through.

Jack Harlow turned onto the path toward Lisa's apartment building. From out of the dark stepped a huge man without an ounce of fat. His arms bulging. Tattoos ran up and down the sides — and across the chest, beneath an open leather vest. He grinned with yellow teeth. One eyebrow was lower than the other and there was no other hair on his head. Silver through his nose, lining his earlobes, studs under his lip. Around his neck, he wore a black dog collar with inch long spikes; more were grafted onto the knuckles of his left hand like claws.

He inhaled, expanding his broad chest, raising his shoulders and lifting his fists to fight. "Nice night, ain't it?"

Normally, Jack could walk right past him, brush by, exchange a few words if absolutely necessary. But tonight, Jack didn't think it'd be so easy. There wasn't anyone else to play victim.

"So, you *watch*," the man said, lifting the higher eyebrow and narrowing the other. "And they think *I'm* the freak."

"What do you want?"

The thing — *ogre* — laughed humorlessly. He reached up, grabbed one of his tattoos — a dagger — and ripped it from his skin. The dagger — metal, not ink — came away with a sticky slapping sound. It was twice as long as the tat had been.

On his other arm, a fanged snake twisted around his thick bicep. He tore it free. It writhed around his hand, black, hissing, venom dripping from its mouth, eyes intent on Jack.

It was Jack's turn to laugh. "Like you need those."

The ogre shrugged. "I like my toys." He pulled the snake-arm back, swung it forward, and shot the end of the snake like a whip.

Jack jumped aside as it snapped. The snake returned to the ogre's hand, but its eyes never left Jack.

"I eat punks like you," the ogre said. "Pick the gristle from my teeth with your bones."

"Appetizing," Jack said.

The ogre swung the snake-whip again, closer, almost getting him. His grin widened as Jack almost stumbled.

Jack couldn't fight it. The man was easily two feet taller and two feet broader, and could probably lift Jack with his pinky finger. There were more weapon-tattoos for him to grab: spikes, dragons, demonic faces.

Jack had only one option. He ran.

He took off to the left, away from Lake Eola and toward the street. He hopped a low hedge, trampled some flowers, and ran between the trees. It wasn't forest-thick here, mostly open spaces near the edge of downtown, so he couldn't hide. He hoped whatever the ogre had gained in muscle, it lost in speed. When Jack glanced back, as he reached the street, the ogre lumbered after him.

Not slowly enough.

Magnolia Avenue was ahead. The trees and houses gave way to buildings and alleys. He put some space between them and halved the distance to the street.

"Wanna party?" a woman asked. He hadn't seen her there, on the side of the road near the corner. Huge breasts, short skirt, bleached blonde hair. She opened her blouse, revealing gnashing teeth on the tips of her breasts. "Free for you tonight, sugar."

Jack ran into the street, heedless of the traffic — which was light. Someone screeched on their brakes. A horn honked. A Lexus swerved, narrowly missing him.

On the other side, Jack looked back. The prostitute smiled and blew pink bubblegum bubbles. The ogre ran into the street — and into the path of a semi.

Jack hadn't seen the truck, either. Its brakes locked. Its horn screamed. It never had a chance to turn before crashing into the ogre.

The truck shuddered with the impact. Bones cracked audibly. The ogre split open down the side. He landed on his face, tumbled and rolled a good fifty feet. Dagger and snake were thrown aside. Blood poured from his arm and face, along his ribs and leg. His entire left side had been demolished.

The truck managed to stop without losing control, but the car behind it smashed into it. The airbag deployed. A moment later, drivers of both car and truck stumbled out of their vehicles.

The hooker, still visible, breasts exposed, teeth champing, popped her bubble gum.

Jack ran down the street, one or two blocks, checking over his shoulder to make sure the ogre never rose and the prostitute stayed on her corner. Finally, panting, he stopped to catch his breath.

2.

Lost him.

Nick Hunter had run after Jack. Still unsure of whether or not to shoot, he ran with gun in hand and the relative certainty he'd be shooting the big, leather-clad monster of a man, but he never got the chance.

Distracted by the big man's being run down, Nick lost sight of Jack. Up and down the street in either direction, he saw nothing but a growing crowd wanting to get a better look at the abomination sprawled across two lanes. Blood pooled beneath the thing. He looked unlikely to get up. That didn't mean anything. His dagger had clattered under one of the cars on either side of the road. Maybe the snake continued the chase.

A number of people rushed forward, or out of their cars, to see the thing in the street and gape at the dent it left in the truck. The driver was shaking, leaning on the side of his vehicle.

Near Nick, a prostitute — a little out of her regular neighborhood, apparently — twirled hair in one hand and pink bubblegum in the other. She looked up and down Nick, smiled big, then looked down at her own cleavage. "Wanna?"

Nick shook his head. "Sorry, hon. Not my type."

"Fuck you," she said, turning back to the scene in the street.

He hadn't followed Jack out of some desire to help, nor out of curiosity — not about Jack, anyhow. He understood enough. If he thought too much about it, he wanted information off that computer. Types. Methods of elimination. The dark, obviously, had kept secrets from Nick — secrets he could find in that tiny black box. And in the back of his mind, he felt an urge to follow, an unnatural instinct thrust upon him from outside. He didn't understand it. Follow, stalk, hurt, kill. He didn't have to obey, not all the way; but the compulsion could not be ignored.

At the first sign of flashing lights, Nick tucked his gun away. The cruiser stopped behind the semi.

If Nick couldn't follow him, he at least knew where Jack was headed.

3.

Jack had run four blocks before the truck demolished the ogre, four blocks away from Lisa and deeper into a dark that surrounded him now. This street wasn't well lit. Houses lined both sides. Behind him, downtown disappeared behind trees that canopied the street. Very little moonlight reached him.

Fences and hedges fronted some houses and apartments. Only a few cars were parked on the cobblestone street. Jack walked in the middle, away from corners, hiding places, and surprises. It had been too interesting a night already.

Leaves rustled in the wind. Cars on other streets sounded like a low, distant murmur. The laptop, thin as it was, felt heavy. There was still a chill on the air. "Still with me?"

"What was that?" the ghost asked.

"Ogre," Jack said. "I think."

"Like, with a club?"

"Almost," Jack said.

"And a snake? I thought I heard a snake."

"What do you hear now?" Jack asked.

After a moment, she said, "Nothing."

"Would you let me know if you do?" Jack asked. "I don't much like surprises."

Silence, then: "Don't you want to know who I am?"

Jack blinked. "What?"

"Who I am," she said. "I mean, you know I'm a ghost. That I was stuck in that motel room until you came along."

"I didn't free you," Jack said.

"No, but you told me how to escape."

"Did I?"

"Go to the light, you said. Except, I can't see, so I followed the warmth. Your warmth." She paused. "Don't you want to know who I am? How I got there?"

Jack thought about it a moment. *Not really,* he wanted to say, but he couldn't. She'd started to become a person to him, more than just part of the darkness. He didn't want to know her. He didn't want the attachment. But it was too late. She was worse than a wink, worse than the ghost in that damned bar trying to tell him stories — but not as bad as the things that wanted him dead. "Can it wait?"

"It's not like I'm going anywhere," she said. "But you can at least ask my name."

When he didn't answer, she said, "Come on, ask who I am."

Jack shook his head. If she had a name, something more than just *the blind ghost girl*, she would be real. He wasn't sure it was a good idea. "What's your name?"

She giggled. "I'm Claire. Claire Winters. Pleased to meet you."

"Hi, Claire," Jack said.

As they talked, he walked. He looked up and down every road he passed, watched driveways and carports, checked windows for silhouettes. He paid careful attention to the movement of shadows.

At Lake Avenue, which was way too small to be called an avenue, Jack turned north again, back toward Lisa's apartment and the lake.

He wouldn't normally expect to see anything else; tonight, in fact, had been the most active ever: imp, hunter, zombie, ogre, even the hooker — and Claire Winters with him every step of the way. But he hadn't *witnessed* things tonight; he'd participated. He expected more. The night was too young, the dark too ominous. Until he reached Lisa's apartment, he wouldn't feel safe.

Not safe was a new sensation for Jack Harlow.

The breeze, at his back, carried a sudden chill. He glanced over his shoulder, not slowing. A minivan on the side of the road. A mailbox. Oaks. A low wooden fence. Bushes. And a shadow, yes, a slippery, slithering shade, almost human in shape. Translucent, with coal-like eyes.

Anyone other than Jack would have missed it.

It flowed without sound, drifting without regard to the wind's direction.

"What is it?" Claire asked.

Jack stopped walking. Narrowed his eyes. It was almost tall, almost broad, nearly solid, and almost on top of him.

"I'm getting tired of this," Jack told the dark.

The mass rolled forward, thicker than the dark around it, deeper than shadows.

It reminded Jack of Edgar Allen Poe: *Deep into that darkness peering, long I stood there wondering, fearing, Doubting, dreaming dreams no mortal ever dared to dream before.* Jack now knew what it was like to be stared down by the abyss. The depth of the darkness, the solidity, the cold, the gloom — it hurt, and it awed and frightened him.

Run, Jack told himself, but his will was not strong enough to make his legs move. *Go.*

"It's so cold," Claire said. Jack felt her shivering. He closed his eyes and prepared for the worst.

For a long while, nothing happened, as though time had stretched infinitely. No life flashed before Jack's eyes, just images of Lisa. Their time together was short, but it had been full of potential. She was the only happiness he'd known since the night he turned seventeen.

He had no expectations of death, nor certainty that it would come. The cold crept around him, pricked his skin, caressed him like a lover — a deeper, harsher cold than the ghost Claire. It enveloped him slowly, slipping between fingers and through his lips, under his eyelids, into his nostrils and ears, into every pore of his skin. It slipped under his clothes, coating him. In his hair like fingers, under his toenails. It coated his tongue, his wrists, his chest. It touched every cell, every molecule, every ion that made Jack what he was, and siphoned him out of himself. Strength ebbed. Consciousness wavered. And the cold intensified.

Hours might have passed. Seconds. Years. The air around him shimmered, threatening to knock him over, but he was frozen. He opened his eyes, best as he could, as the cold seeped away.

Claire.

She stood, back to him, arms locked around the shadow. They struggled, dancing, wrestling, neither fully visible but both solidifying in the cold.

"Run!" Claire said.

Jack still couldn't move. The ice left gradually. His muscles were achy and stiff. Ghost and shadow melded together, joining at the hands, the hips, even the mouths locked in an eternal kiss as their bodies crystalized together.

The shadow's scream was so high-pitched, Jack heard nothing but had to cover his ears because of the pain. Windows on nearby cars splintered. In the distance, in every direction, dogs started barking — and wolves. Bats took flight. Shadows receded. The shade, and Claire

Winters, became a solid thing. They dropped to the street, no longer floating, all sense of cold gone from Jack's body.

He'd been half an inch from death.

Where they fell, their legs crumbled like dust. The rest of their distorted bodies began to break apart. Chunks that hit the ground puffed into gray dust and dissipated.

"Claire?" Jack asked.

No answer. A section of the ghost/shadow's body split away, shattering, and the rest fell to one side, disintegrating on impact.

Jack stepped back, his muscles timid but working. Nothing of Claire remained. The shadows around him were normal, albeit dark and thick. The air was warm, almost hot. She'd sacrificed herself for him — but he wasn't worth it. He hadn't earned it. It was a debt he could never repay.

No longer content to walk, to wait for whatever else lurked in the dark, Jack ran. His first steps were stumbling; his muscles had almost given up on life.

A sudden fear struck him: if these things attacked Jack, how did Lisa fare, alone in her apartment?

With all his belief, every ounce and fiber of it, Jack knew he was the target, not Lisa. She was fine, sleeping and dreaming beautiful things, daytime things, puppies and dandelions,
windmills and roses, diamonds and seashores. Logically, there was no reason to go after her. *He* was the watcher, the eyes in the night — more than that, a *DarkWalker*. She was innocent.

He ran faster.

CHAPTER NINE

1.

Halfway to the apartment, Nick Hunter paused. He was on the sidewalk, same side of the street as the lake, when the smell assaulted him.

He hadn't been looking for it. He sought a human quarry. But there was no mistaking that horrendous vampiric stink. Most would attribute it to gas or dog shit in the gutter. Nick had lived with that smell for years.

He looked left and right, then scanned the tree limbs above him. So strong a smell meant the beast was near. Slowly, Nick reached for his gun. He heard only the crickets and the wind. He traced that stench toward the lake.

Amid a sparse plot of trees, a vampire, crouching alongside the lake, examined something on the water. It was male, ashen but not the alabaster of the type he'd slain the night before, with a full head of hair and decked out all in black. Ears like a cat's, folded back, twitching.

Nick aimed his gun. Certain vampires were more resilient than others. A gunshot gave him plenty of time to stake the Nosferatu beasts; this type, a prince of a man complete with cape and, likely, a false Transylvanian accent, generally did not fall so easily.

One of its ears snapped suddenly back and its muscles tensed. Slowly, it turned its head. When their eyes met, Nick pulled the trigger.

The bullet struck the vampire's forehead. The force knocked it backwards, into the lake with a splash.

"Shit." Nick surged forward, drawing a stake.

The vampire floated on its back, next to the zombie's body. Its eyes were open, looking up at Nick, and its teeth were bared. Hideously deformed canines dominated its smile.

Nick leapt into the water, stake first, and plunged the wood into the beast's heart. A fountain of black blood erupted.

The water, here, was only thigh deep. Nick dragged the vampire back to the edge and, with some effort, shoved it over the artificial lake wall and onto the grass before climbing out himself. His lighter started on the second try.

The vampire flared. Despite being wet, it was quickly reduced to ash.

Nick looked around and saw that he'd been seen — by owls, rats, cockroaches, even a cat. They'd paused, all headed in a singular direction, and had turned their heads to watch.

"It's done," Nick told them.

They didn't listen, didn't acknowledge him, and continued when they were ready — cat first, but not in any sort of procession. Knowing where they headed, Nick followed.

2.

Not much further.

The apartment's vestibule came into view as Jack rounded the corner. Forty feet. Thirty. Maybe less.

A black limo had parked in the road, directly in his path. The rear door opened and a blond man beckoned with one finger. "Quickly."

"No." Jack raced around the side of the limo, over the curb and under the awning of the apartment. The car door closed, but Jack did not look back. He keyed his way past the double glass doors and went to the stairs. He was tired, but he wasn't going to give away his destination via the floor indicators of an elevator.

Large black numbers labeled each landing in the staircase. He burst through the door on five, half expecting the corridor to be crowded with ghouls and goblins.

Nothing.

Emotions raced through him. *Fear, anxiety* — was Lisa safe? *Regret* and *guilt* at Claire's second death — she'd wanted to tell her story and he'd refused it. *Anger*, too, but without direction. Something, someone, was responsible for this shift. *Relief* at having reached Lisa's apartment. The door was shut tight, locked, just as he'd left it. Was it a sanctuary? No. He'd be no safer inside...and Lisa would be endangered by his arrival.

Jack paused a moment to catch his breath. He looked right and left, left and right, then up, down, and behind him, checking for sudden apparitions and silent arrivals. None. No one. Nothing. He wiped a line of sweat from his brow, took a deep breath, and inserted the key.

3.

After Jack left, Lisa Sparrow had waited, then stared out the window a while, tried reading through her dream journals, and finally settled into a mindless exercise routine. She was in the middle of a long, low stretch when she heard the key in the door. Her stomach rose to her throat. Her heart pounded so hard, she thought it might break her ribs.

She rose too quickly, almost losing balance. She wiped her face with a kitchen towel. There were only two possibilities: Jack, or something else — not *someone*. She no longer feared the unknown man in the shadows, just the shadows themselves.

Jack Harlow entered, locking the door behind him. He smiled when he saw Lisa, but she caught something before that: fear. Whether it was fear of what was outside, or of Lisa (and all the associated possibilities), she didn't know. She shared both, but neither would overwhelm her. Not now. With her blood pumping, adrenaline and endorphins flowing, dopamine and serotonin, nothing could bring her down.

He hugged her. Clutched and clung to her.

"It's going to be a long night, isn't it?"

"It already is."

When Jack released the embrace, grudgingly, he set his laptop on the kitchen counter and turned it on. He opened screens, scrolled through them, searched for particular pieces of text. *Imp.* That's what he looked for first. Then he tried other searches, Lisa looking over his shoulder.

The words on the screen began to gel, to make a weird sort of sense they should not have. This wasn't a horror movie. Ghosts existed in films and books and campfire stories, not in the modern world. Lisa never truly disbelieved; it wasn't hard now to accept that things like phantoms and — *zombies?* — existed. But what was Jack Harlow, that he kept this on a computer?

"What are you looking for?" she asked.

Jack paused, but didn't answer immediately. She understood, too: how to explain what he was, what he was searching for. She had her own secrets. She put a hand on his arm, kissed him lightly, and whispered, "It's okay. I don't care *how.*"

"I don't know how," Jack finally said. "It — it's a long story, I think, but I don't know all of it."

"The short version, then."

Jack nodded. Swallowed. Lowered his eyes. "You know how, when it gets dark, shadows obscure what you see, hide things that tend not to even be there?" Lisa nodded. "I see through those shadows. I see the dark."

"In the dark?"

"That, too," Jack said.

Lisa rested her head against his shoulder. "I won't pretend to understand," she said, "but I do. A little."

"The thing is," Jack said, "they've always seen me, too, and ignored me. Like I was *supposed* to see, and they didn't really care."

"And now?"

"Now," Jack said, "I'm a target."

"And me?" Lisa asked. Jack turned back to the computer. "And me?" she asked again.

"The catalyst," he said.

No.

That couldn't be right. Lisa understood him completely, if not the details. Her life had changed when Jack Harlow stepped into it — but could she have changed his life *that* drastically? No way. Not a chance.

"It's got to be something else."

"Something," Jack said, "but I don't have it."

"The thing that attacked me?" She shuddered; just mentioning it revived images of chomping teeth and razor claws. Cuts all across her body burned in remembrance.

Jack nodded. "I've never seen anything like it, or a lot of the things I've seen tonight."

Lisa smiled. "Not all bad, I hope."

"No," he said, stepping closer to kiss her. "Not all bad."

"So now what?"

Jack shook his head, "I don't know. I don't think you're safe with me, and I don't think I'm safe in your apartment."

"Then where?"

"Different places for different things," Jack said. "I don't know of any one place to hide from everything." He sighed. It wasn't much of a stretch to say he'd been hiding, running, from himself, from the thing he was. "I don't really want to spend my life in hiding."

"Then don't," Lisa said. "You've been seeing these things for long enough, haven't you? Don't you know how to fight them?"

Jack nodded once, but closed his eyes. "Some."

Someone — or something — knocked on the door.

4.

Nick Hunter returned to the apartment building.. He picked the lock to get inside.

Nick rode the elevator, letting the doors open on every floor until he noticed a spot of blood on the tile.

The trail didn't lead specifically to a door, unfortunately, but left him just five from which to choose. Inside one, a radio played softly.

He knocked. He didn't have to. The locks here were simple, the doors flimsy.

Jack opened the door cautiously. Nick could have pushed at the first sign of movement, smashing Jack's face and maybe knocking him out. Despite the urge, he didn't.

"Hunter," Jack said.

"You got lucky with that truck." Without waiting for an invitation, he stepped in and shut the door.

"Who?" the woman asked. The thing hadn't scratched her up too badly. She might not scar.

"Nick Hunter. We never got a proper introduction downstairs."

"Lisa Sparrow."

Jack locked the door. "I hate to say this, but I'm not safe to be around."

"I noticed," Nick said. He winked at Lisa. "I thought I'd steal some of the glory."

"An errant zombie, ogre, a living shadow," Jack said. "That's just a beginning. There was a ghost, too. Claire. She's gone now. Took out the shadow."

"You have allies," Nick said. "Good."

"*Had*," Jack said. "I don't know what to do next."

"Isn't that obvious?" Lisa asked.

Nick glanced at her, fairly certain of what she was about to say. Jack asked, "What?"

"Stay here," Lisa said. "Wait until the sun comes up. It's…" She looked to a clock. "It's after two."

"Almost five hours before sunrise," Nick said. "Long time."

"First," Jack said, "I need to know something." He looked at Nick with steady eyes, fearlessly, a man who had seen too much to be frightened by it.

Nick said. "Of course I'll help."

"Help?" Lisa asked.

"I'm a hunter," Nick said. "Makes my job easier, if they come to me."

"I haven't seen a vampire yet," Jack said.

"I've decided to expand."

"You said you didn't like my spotlight."

Nick nodded toward the open computer. "These other things out there, I know nothing about them."

"And you just want to kill them all?" Lisa asked.

Nick glared at her. "The things I kill, if given half a chance, would suck you dry in a way you might or might not enjoy and leave you for dead. But you wouldn't be dead, not exactly. You'd wake with that same insatiable thirst. They're predators, and we — we're the prey." He grinned. "I need to be better prepared."

5.

Jack Harlow hadn't considered his computer an object of importance. His files carried data on more than two hundred species indigenous to the dark, including weaknesses. He'd learned some of it from various websites, but there were only a few of those he trusted.

Lisa gave him the Wi-Fi password. Someday, he'd need something more mobile than a laptop.

"Some weapons work on a number of things," Jack told Nick. "What kind of sword is that?"

Nick the blade from a sheath hidden under his jacket. "Knife," he said. "Silver blade. Marble handle."

"Silver?" Lisa asked.

"Inherited," Nick said.

"Silver's good," Jack said. "Useful against several types of vampires, lycanthropes, other things. That zombie downstairs, any blade would've worked." He glanced at the screen, called up the website. "It was beheading that mattered there."

"Nice to know," Nick said. "Bullets are silver, too."

"Good."

"I've got more weapons in my truck."

Jack clicked a few buttons, typed *imp*, and waited.

"Damn." No results. He tried another source, then a third, finding nothing useful. Jack shut the computer. "This isn't helping."

"What, then?" Nick asked.

Jack thought a moment. Claire had entered his life just before all this started; what else had there been? Two nights ago was so far away. There was the ash stalker snorting his victim; the Asian vampire winking at him; and the ghost in the bar.

"Stories," Jack said. "I've got to go hear a story."

"I'm going with you," Lisa said.

"No."

"Yes."

"It's too dangerous," he said.

"No more so than sitting here," Lisa said. "Anyway, you might need protection."

"I'll handle that," Nick said.

Her eyes never left Jack. "From him."

Jack sighed. "I don't know what else might be out there."

"But you've already led them here," Lisa told him. "Pointed them straight to me. I'm not going to wait for them."

Nick said, "I work alone."

"You're already not alone."

"Stop," Jack said.

Everyone looked at him. He inhaled, long and deep, making them wait before turning to Nick. "Can you give her the knife," Jack said. "Arm me, too, when we get a chance. It's me they're after."

After a long moment, Nick shrugged. He flipped the knife in his hand and, holding the blade, gave it to Lisa.

"Good," Jack said. "Hunter, how well can you see through the dark?"

"I see fine," Nick said, "but I can smell a vampire a block away."

6.

Lisa Sparrow had ceased to exist.

The woman she'd been had died. That Lisa would not have gone off into the night with two total strangers (okay, *one* total stranger, and one almost stranger with dark secrets). But what else could she do, let Jack go off on his own?

If he left, there'd be nothing for her to do but wonder. Think. Worry. Imagine. One thing she didn't need was to be left alone with her imagination, not after that thing — that *imp*.

No, better to risk the night and maybe die *knowing*, rather than waiting. He might return in the morning, battle-weary but alive, or not at all — or worse, months from now, beaten, changed into something unimaginable.

She wasn't about to let things just happen around her.

The knife felt strangely comfortable in her hand. Heavy, but cold. It extracted the heat from her fingers. Rather than leaving her numb, it heightened her senses. It was like walking within one of her dreams. Surreal and absurd. Weighty.

She watched every shadow.

She listened to every sound — as few as there were.

They might be surrounded by all manner of animal, person, and unknown. Even the rats — she saw three of them (she'd never seen three, not at one time, not out in the open) sitting and staring, their long gray bodies almost black, their tales naked, their eyes steady.

Nothing moved. Yet. It was a matter of time. She'd entered a world that existed on the fringes of her own. She would follow Jack to the corners of the earth, and he might actually go there.

She tried to clear her mind, tried to concentrate on their mission. What was it, exactly? To listen to a story? She suspected the storyteller would be a psychic, a shaman, perhaps a Voodoo priestess from New Orleans. It was all real now. Bigfoot, aliens, super government conspiracies, Dracula, even the gods of Mt. Olympus. In the other world, where the former Lisa Sparrow lived, none of this existed outside of fairy tales and dreams.

Eyes wide, the new Lisa Sparrow dismissed nothing as fancy. Dreams were visions, mirrors portals, and frogs princes. The rainbow, should she live to see another, led directly to a leprechaun and his gold. And Jack Harlow, who had come not entirely unpredicted into her life, became not just a lover but a guide to all the things of the dark.

CHAPTER TEN

1.

This was the right thing to do. The compulsion to hurt Jack was unnatural. Nick Hunter walked with this couple like he belonged. In fact, he had more in common with Jack than anyone else alive.

The hairs on the back of his neck stood on end. His heart pounded. From every direction, eyes were trained on them, following, stalking. This wasn't merely hunted or even hounded, but marked and exposed.

The quality of the night had changed. Clouds veiled the moon and glowed with the reflected lights of the city, yet the dark tightened and the air thinned. The staccato of their feet bounced off the buildings.

Silence undercut the sounds they made. An occasional car passed on a cross street. The fountain splashed, but distantly. To Nick's heightened senses, their heartbeats rocked the night; no other creature made a sound.

Nick glanced over his shoulder. The apartment building was a couple of blocks back now. Did something stand on its roof, only to step away when Nick noticed?

The sidewalk was clear. Unless something crouched behind a parked car, there were no immediate threats.

He looked down, checking the computer in the corner of his eye. Jack carried it in a bag that offered little protection. Anyone who wanted the machine could simply take it — slice Jack's wrist and take the whole hand, if necessary. Nick pushed back against the intrusive urge. It came from outside him, so he could resist it.

The crowd where the ugly tattooed man met the truck had thinned. Most of the police were gone, and also the truck, though the mangled car remained.

"Where, exactly, are we going?" Lisa asked.

"A bar," Jack said.

"They're all closed by now." Lisa glanced at her wrist, but there was no watch.

"Doesn't matter," Jack said. "The man I'm looking for won't necessarily be inside. Just *attached*."

"This helps, how?" Nick asked.

Jack hesitated before answering. "I'm not sure it will."

2.

Briefly, Jack Harlow thought they'd reach the bar unaccosted. With the lake behind them, and eyes in windows instead of trees, they passed a series of one-way streets. Rounding a corner onto Orange, they were within sight of the bar.

It was too late in the morning, too long after closing, for the psychic to sit outside. Only the breeze occupied the street — and a layer of darkness, inappropriate even to Jack's eyes. He detected an aroma of jasmine, vanilla, cinnamon — then decay. Unmistakable, overpowering, and awful. Rot like cabbage unattended, dead rats, congealed blood.

Nick halted. Sniffed. "Vampire?"

"No," Jack said.

"Death," Nick said, drawing his gun. "The city reeks of it."

Lisa coughed and backed against the glass wall of a shoe store. "You live with this all the time?"

Jack scanned the windows across the street, above a restaurant. Under its awning, in the shadows of its doorway, stood a black man in a black suit. He had a big shiny coin in his left hand.

Nick, seeing him, aimed.

Staring back with colorless eyes, the man flipped the coin once, smiled broadly, and stepped out from under the awning.

Three lanes separated them. No cars. No people. Just two broken white lines.

"*Vaudoux*," Jack realized.

"Indeed," said the man.

"What?" Nick whispered.

"Like a witch doctor," Jack said. "A sorcerer. From Haiti."

"Well, not quite," the man said, pocketing the coin. "Santo Domingo, actually." His accent was thick, almost French, almost Spanish, clipped with a touch of British. He was old. Well-traveled. "Please, put down your weapon."

Nick did not lower his aim. "You smell like a vampire."

"Actually, I don't," the man said. "Incense, maybe. Jasmine. Spices. But I smell it, too, my friend."

"Friend?" Lisa asked.

"You would usually ignore me," Jack said, taking one step into the street.

The vaudoux nodded.

"But not tonight?"

"Not tonight," he said. "Apparently, no."

"Why not?"

"Your glow."

"What?"

"Your aura, you might say," the vaudoux said. "It screams to be noticed. Seen. Touched. Ripped."

"I don't want that," Jack said.

"I can't help you. But I had to see for myself, of course."

"Why can't you help?" Jack asked. "If there are rules to all this, haven't they changed?"

"Rules," the vaudoux said, shaking his head, "never change, and have no place between us. I cannot help because..." He shrugged. "Because I cannot. There is no spell to remove your aura, it's what you are, who you are. It demands to be seen. And it warps the dark around you." He flicked the coin across the street. Jack caught it with one hand. "I was already close," he said. "But there are others, not so near, who will come. Others, not so strong as I, who will be unable to resist your magnetism."

"Is that a threat?" Nick asked.

"A warning," the vaudoux said.

Jack examined the coin. It was silver, solid, unadorned on either side.

"Magic," the vaudoux said, "comes in many forms. Shapes, sizes, are unimportant, Mr. Jack." He laughed, a quick, hearty Caribbean laugh, as smoke swirled around his feet and snaked up his body, until only white teeth and eyes were visible. His laugh echoed even as the smoke dispersed. The vaudoux was gone.

"Witchdoctor?" Lisa asked.

"You've seen him before?" Nick asked.

"Him, no," Jack said.

But Jack Harlow had glimpsed a vaudoux once before, briefly, in Miami — South Beach, actually — standing on a balcony of one of the art deco houses. He'd held a fresh human skull in one hand and sprinkled powders over it. He chanted so quietly, the skull could not have heard. A woman walked on the beach, not two hundred yards away, beautiful skin, black as shadows and braided hair falling to her waist. Possibly a model, once, she was no longer alive, not completely, but enthralled. When the vaudoux completed his spell, the woman — a kind of zombie — stopped in mid step. She crossed the street, passed one café, and went straight to a man calling customers into a restaurant. "Lovely lady like you," he said with a thick island accent, "ought not be wasted on a fine young night like this."

"Ought not," she said, before kissing him. It was a long, lingering kiss, hot and wet, the kind a man would kill for — or die for. She walked away as his mouth foamed and his eyes bulged. Sweat ran from every pore in his body. He swung his head. Lips curled back, drying, flaking. Spots mottled his skin. The people near him scattered, like they might catch the plague. He stumbled to one leg. Agony etched his face. Smoke streamed from his eyes like tears. Finally, he saw the vaudoux on the rooftop. He opened and closed his mouth, trying to speak but his teeth dropped out. He doubled over, clutching his stomach, and fell face down to the sidewalk.

The vaudoux had lowered the skull and stood perfectly still. The victim sizzled, smoked, burned, and melted. His skin ran like water. Eventually, he was just a stain on the street; not even a tooth remained by which to identify him.

No one had seen the woman — or the vaudoux. No one but Jack Harlow.

3.

"His stink's still here," Nick said, not resting the gun. Maybe he thought the vaudoux had turned himself invisible, but the smell came from somewhere else. Something else.

Jack glanced at Lisa. She tried to smile at him. Jack returned it, took her hand and squeezed. "We're not alone," he said.

Stupid thing to say. They hadn't been alone since leaving the apartment. All manner of creatures had focused on them. Every corner was dangerous. The children of the night were many and they were everywhere.

Further up the road, beyond the ghost's club, a pair of men stood at a corner: thin and wiry, one wearing glasses, the other holding back a beast on a leash. Six legs, the head of a lizard and the body of a — was it a beetle? Maybe a scarab — and a snake-like tail, it salivated, straining at the leash that bit into its neck.

"Stories," Lisa reminded him.

"Right." Jack turned his attention to the blackened windows less than a hundred yards down the road.

Something dropped from the sky.

Hands black as coal, claws, no visible face under its hood, its cloak was like smoke folding into itself, shifting in the breeze. It screeched, turned, and swooped at Jack. The high pitch shattered the shoe store's window. Lisa fell backwards. Nick readjusted his stance and fired three shots into the wraith without effect.

It hovered over the ground, directly in front of Jack. The robes swarmed behind it.

Jack stepped back, stumbling, held by the wraith's gaze. Its eyes — there were no irises, no pupils, no whites, no sockets for them — its eyes reflected Jack. In the reflection, he screamed, he pounded his fists in the air, he banged on an invisible box like a mime in excruciating pain and fear.

Jack barely felt his feet leave the ground. Barely heard more gunshots and Lisa calling his name. Her hand swiped his leg as she tried to grab him.

He stared at himself — reflected, distorted, agonized.

"Do not be afraid," a cold, whispery voice said, a slick, slithering, nasty voice that pierced Jack's head, smashed his sinuses, rooted into his eyes, and dug into his chest. Jack's reflection screamed and screamed soundlessly.

"I will ease your pain," the wraith said. Oil. Sticky and disgusting. Like acid, its voice seeped into Jack's skin, under his muscles, into pinholes in his bones.

Jack's reflection cried, tears racing down his cheek, the whites of his eyes burning red. Blood dripped from his nose and sprayed from his shrieking mouth.

"Do something!" Lisa screamed, trying to grab him again.

Jack closed his eyes. Stop looking, stop feeling, stop listening to the thing.

"I can end your suffering."

He reached toward those eyes with both hands. Grabbed them — nothing to grab but smoke and dust and air — and crushed them in his grip.

The wraith screeched. The two lurched sideways, striking the brick wall hard enough to shake Jack's bones.

Opening his eyes again, Jack saw the wraith's skeletal face, the holes where eyes might have been (his own hands there, squeezing), teeth missing in its grin. It was a smoky, insubstantial skull, and there was no reflection in its eyes.

To be certain, Jack shut his again and yanked backwards.

With a screech, the wraith released him.

They might have been hundreds of feet into the sky, over buildings or trees or roads. Jack had no way of knowing, and no chance to brace himself for impact. He bounced on the sidewalk.

"Jack!" Lisa called, immediately kneeling at his side, hand around the back of his neck, lifting his head. Three more gunshots.

With one final screech, the wraith was gone.

Jack struggled for breath — the fall had knocked it out of him. He looked up at Lisa, smiled, touched her cheek, concentrated on breathing before saying anything.

Nick said, "I don't think I hurt it."

No, he hadn't. Wraiths were insubstantial, a kind of ghost gone wrong. And empathic, apparently; Jack hadn't known that. He didn't know a lot of things. He'd watched, listened, recorded, but never investigated.

"You're okay," Lisa said. "You're okay, there's no blood, you'll be fine. Right? You'll be alright?"

Jack nodded once. "I will."

"What was it?" Nick asked. "Smelled like a vampire."

"No," Jack said. "It smelled like death."

4.

Jack needed another moment. The fall hadn't hurt him, but the wraith had frightened him. There'd been a moment when he expected to die. He'd felt the pain of his reflection, burning and boring through him. Had that been a future the wraith offered? *I will ease your pain. I will end your suffering.*

Jack closed his eyes. Inhaled deep. Exhaled slowly. Controlled.

The dark lied. The creatures of the night were liars, thieves, murderers. The wraith had not meant to save him. He'd seen wraiths in action before. They skinned and flayed their victims, and left bloodied broken skeletons. Wraiths came from the depths of despair. It was true, their victims felt no more pain — not after the wraith left them — but the agony, even in reflection, had been as much as he could withstand. Over the course of what, a minute? Wraiths could spend hours peeling to its victim's core.

Jack had avoided that fate, but what awaited?

CHAPTER ELEVEN

1.

Lisa Sparrow held Jack's hand, held his head, said nothing about the tears trickling from his eye. He was right; it had smelled like death. She'd recognize that odor next time. Maybe she'd be able to *do* something, even if the hunter could not.

She didn't know what the new Lisa Sparrow would be like. Stronger? She'd never been weak. Smarter? She'd never been dumb. More aware, maybe. Eyes open. Alert. *Conscious.* Like Jack and Nick, and even that smoky beast, she now belonged to the night.

It hadn't been the teeth and claws that changed Lisa's life, but Jack. The moment they'd met, everything had changed.

She hated to think she might be the catalyst that had endangered him. He was a watcher, not a victim. Maybe she couldn't see everything, but she'd seen the vaudoux, and the smoke, and the imp — more than enough for any sane, rational person. She *was* sane, and rational, but accepting.

Jack opened his eyes again. He looked straight at her and gave a weak smile. "Stories," he said.

"Right." She helped Jack to his feet, then retrieved the knife she'd dropped at the shattered window. No more fancy pumps for her, no stiletto heels, nothing for going out. Sensible shoes so she could run, jump, fight

The future stretched before her like a blank canvas, wiped clear of the mundane.

Now, she saw the sentinels more clearly: in the corner of an upstairs apartment window, a cat watched them. A bird upon the flagpole. Faces in the alleys, belonging not just to the homeless who had lined the path along the lake. Exposure had made her aware of things she'd previously ignored.

"You okay?" Jack asked.

"Me?" Lisa kissed him lightly. "I'm not the one falling like a stone."

"I hate to break this up, kids," Nick said, "but we ought to keep moving."

2.

Nick Hunter checked his watch. Less than two hours till sunrise.

Jack led the way to a club. All such places were closed. Late-night eateries were dark, gates were rolled down over storefronts, doors locked. The last stray customers were home asleep, dreaming or nightmaring.

"Well?" Jack said. He wasn't talking to Nick, or even to Lisa, but to the ghost. "You said you had stories to tell," Jack said. "Would blow my mind." Emotionless. No fear, no excitement, nothing. Admirable, Nick thought.

The ghost, the other half of the conversation, remained invisible to Nick Hunter. Still, Nick kept a hand on his gun, and didn't let his gaze rest on either of his companions.

The rooftops seemed empty, nearby windows clear. Here, in the heart of an empty downtown, every sound echoed. A pebble pushed by a roach resounded like an avalanche. Every noise attracted Nick's attention.

The next attack could come from anywhere. It might even be a vampire.

He saw maybe the trace of a figure in the blackened window, a hint, but heard no voice. Then, Jack's cool veneer slid into disappointment — and anger.

3.

"What do you mean, it's too late?"

In the window, the ghost seemed like a living photograph, neither whole nor three-dimensional: a pale image shimmering, distorted by imperfections in the glass.

"You've marked yourself," the ghost said. "You didn't just make yourself a target, you slapped on a green, day-glow raincoat that screams *Come and get me* like a fuckin' dinner bell."

"So," Jack said, "are you here to get me?"

"Not interested," the ghost said, "though I've got to admit, the thought has its appeal."

"Really?" Jack didn't like the direction of this conversation, but he needed information.

"Hey, it's your life," the ghost said. "Or death, as it may be." He turned his eyes to Lisa. "She's cute, though not as fine as the lass here the other night."

"No?" Lisa asked.

The ghost raised its eyebrows. "You see me?" He turned his attention to Nick. "And what about you, there, with that stupid expression like someone's about to jump out and go *Boo*, do you see me too?" Nick, however, did not respond. "Guess not. So there's two of you, then. If you really want stories, I can tell you some. Though to be honest..." He paused, looking again at Lisa. "I really hate to spoil a lady's ears."

"Tell me more about this *raincoat*," Jack said.

"Raincoat?" The ghost furrowed his eyebrows. "Ah, yes, that. Just a metaphor. You're attracting, now. Strong pull. You just ain't the same as when we first met. Should've listened to my stories then, maybe you'd have skipped on the big change. You had a slipperiness then, a suggestion of *look away* about you, a flashing red sign that said, *No Touch*. Now, it demands, *Do your worst*."

"What changed me?"

The ghost laughed. "Damned if I know." He had no information for Jack. He only wanted an audience. "Tell you what," the ghost said. "Why don't you come in, pour yourselves a drink, and sit back for a while? I'll tell you about a girl I knew back in…in…well, fuck, who cares what year it was, right? She was gorgeous, that's all that matters. Body to kill." He winked at Lisa. "Like yours, really. Blonder hair, shorter. A fox, I tell you."

Lisa looked at Jack. He said, "Maybe another time."

"C'mon," the ghost said. "Drinks are on the house."

Jack shook his head. "When I've removed the raincoat."

"That, right. Good luck. Never seen anything like it. Almost gives me the strength to get out of this place." He shimmered. "Still stuck. I swear, if you pulled, I mean gave a good, strong tug, you could get me out of here."

"You're not just a ghost," Jack said. "A revenant, right?" No answer. "I imagine you'll be stuck there until you do something about the guy who killed you."

"And what would you know about it?" the ghost asked; his image bubbled and turned like boiling water. "He ain't never been back, never can, he's as dead as I am and enjoying the fuck out of it. So why don't you take your sweet little girlfriend and your paranoid pal and find some other corner of the dark to haunt? This place is mine."

The revenant turned sharply and faded quickly.

Lisa touched Jack's shoulder. Her eyes glistened — or were they his eyes? If the ghost couldn't tell him anything, who could?

"Is it gone?" Nick asked.

"He knew nothing," Jack said. "Which gains me exactly nothing."

"Any other potential fonts of information?"

Jack Harlow, in fact, had no idea what to do next. His life had consisted of wandering. No maps, no destinations. He followed roads. Sometimes, they brought him someplace interesting. Often, they led to the middle of nowhere.

He sometimes believed the roads conspired against him, bringing him to various towns and cities specifically to witness something and write it down, as if the highways had intentions for him.

If a greater mind had a plan for him, a reason for his sight, Jack didn't know it.

The wraith was the first thing he'd actually fought. It had seemed small, what he'd done, but he knew better. Just closing his own eyes, pulling himself away from the suffering of his reflection, had been a feat of willpower.

Sometimes, he knew things he shouldn't. Their methods, their strengths and weaknesses, and fears. He'd known to put out the wraith's eyes, that the zombie's head must be cut. These were instincts, not learned by rote or experience.

But if he walked a predetermined path, nothing indicated his next step.

4.

Nick Hunter shifted his weight from foot to foot. He glanced down the street and toward the rooftops, waiting for something, anything, to strike.

This wasn't his game. He could step out whenever he wanted and walk away. Nothing, absolutely nothing, prevented him from running off. Vicious, rotting, inhuman creatures existed in the dark. The vampires gave Nick plenty of exercise. Did he need more?

"You've been doing this a while," Lisa said to Jack. "I'd think, by now, you would know of someone who can help you."

Jack shook his head. "Mostly, I just see things. They rarely speak to me, and I've never, never approached them."

"Maybe," Lisa said, "that was a mistake."

The stench of death returned: rotting tissue and fresh earth. Nick cleared his throat. "We're about to have company."

"I can't change what I didn't do," Jack said.

This wasn't a vampire smell. It carried a hint of mold and worms. He heard a snapping of bones, like twigs, as the thing came closer.

Nick settled into a low fighting stance and looked everywhere with his gun.

"Maybe we should go," Lisa suggested.

They were nearly twenty paces from the corner. The building obscured view of the cross street.

"Too late," Nick said.

The dead thing rounded the corner. It had followed their path, dragging one foot behind it. A man just a week ago, it was now moist and sludgy. When it came into sight, its putrid odor intensified. Its eyes were dead, coated by a white membrane that contrasted the dirt-encrusted face and body. Its mouth hung open, the jaw broken and teeth missing. Both arms dangled at its sides. Something had eaten away most of its midsection and genitals.

The dead man moved with incredible slowness, pushing one stiff leg out, pulled itself forward.

If it had been a vampire, Nick could hit it between the eyes, in the throat, or in the heart. Everything was exposed. But he couldn't kill a dead thing, even with bullets of silver, and he didn't want to waste them on such a negligible threat.

He stepped back, lowered his gun, and said, "I don't think we have to worry about this one."

Then all hell broke loose.

CHAPTER TWELVE

1.

As soon as Nick's eyes left it, the dead thing *moved*. It was not so slow as it pretended. Suddenly quick and agile, it wrapped a tight, strong hand around Nick's wrist. The skin sloughed a little, but Nick couldn't pull free before it pried his gun loose.

A winged man, with fangs and talons, swooped from the rooftops, passing over Nick, aiming for Jack and Lisa.

Other figures moved, too, but the dead thing demanded Nick's attention. Nick managed to twist his hand free, then kneed the dead man's stomach cavity. Maggots and worms spilled from its mouth. Flies swarmed around its head. Nick punched the thing in the chest. His fist broke through rotted flesh and cracked the sternum. For an infinite, panic-filled moment, Nick couldn't pull his hand free.

2.

Lisa finally screamed when the clay man grabbed her.

She hadn't seen it, didn't see where it had come from. Its hands were soft and malleable, but solid enough to wrap across her chest and yank her backwards — out of the path of the winged man.

With all her strength, and every ounce of self-defense training she'd ever picked up, she elbowed its chest, making a squishy sound. Its hold slackened just enough for Lisa to duck down, slip forward, and spun to face it.

The golem stood at least seven feet tall. Its face had barely been shaped into the idea of a man. It wore the indentation of her elbow.

No mouth had been marked. It could neither speak nor grin. It lunged with both hands, meaning to choke her. Lisa jumped back, just out of its range.

A battalion of rats swarmed at her feet, gray, thick fists, with long naked tails and iridescent red eyes. Most ran past her, entangling her feet; but some climbed her calves. One bit behind her knee. Two fell loose on their own; as she swept more away, another bit her lower thigh.

Then the clay hands found her throat.

3.

Jack ducked to avoid the talons of the winged man.

Jack Harlow had walked in the dark for years. He'd never seen different creatures working together. The dead man lunging at Nick, the golem grabbing Lisa — both mindless automatons, and golems usually worked to protect someone.

When he turned, the were-bat was fully human, except for its claws, those teeth, and bat-like ears. Like any other lycanthropic thing, it was part human but mostly beast; it was unintelligent and primal, driven by instinct. It was vicious and strong and fierce and relentless.

It hissed, grabbing Jack by the throat. Behind the were-bat, there was something else. Something big. It was twice the size of any of them, bigger even than the ogre had been, with burgundy skin, a single horn in its head, yellow cat eyes, and three-fingered hands.

But the were-bat had him. Its fingers ripped the flesh of his neck. Jack fell backwards, pulling the man-like thing on top of him. He lost his breath when he hit the sidewalk. The beast hissed.

4.

The rats came as an organized swarm, a small army, a squadron of which had broken from the rest of the pack to focus on Lisa. A half dozen — *at least* — climbed her, their tiny claws clinging to her jeans and shirt, their teeth — *more teeth* — taking small chunks of flesh. Clay hands tightened around her throat, crushing her windpipe. She kicked, hard, to no avail. Her punches made small, ineffective thuds.

One of the rats reached the clay hands and came at her face. Lisa shook her head violently, losing the rat and loosening the clay grip — but not enough. Another rat chomped on her stomach.

She shoved forward, into the clay golem, throwing it off balance, backwards, and into the wall. The rats that fell never returned, going for their real target: Jack. The golem lost his grip. Lisa wrenched herself free, and hit something on the ground.

5.

Lisa toppled over the were-bat and Jack. The beast took the brunt of her fall, allowing Jack to finally roll free. But even as he reached his feet again, despite the rats swarming around him, he was grabbed from behind. One hand snaked under his arm and around his torso; the other covered his mouth. Her chest pressed to his back, her lips close enough that her breath warmed his ear. She whispered, "Hold on."

Then she jumped.

Gunshots followed. The were-bat hissed, transforming as it, too, leapt into the sky. The golem looked up. The rats, confused, scattered. The red-skinned demon clenched its fists and snarled.

Then Jack couldn't see the street anymore. His captor landed, rough, on the roof, two stories above the street, and pulled him away from the edge.

6.

His hand barely out of the dead man's chest, Nick Hunter threw a crescent kick — raising his leg alongside his opponent and smashing the side of its head hard enough to crack bones. The thing stumbled aside, dazed, dropping Nick's gun.

A second kick snapped the dead man's neck. The head lolled to one side, hanging by threads of rotted flesh. Nick brought up an elbow, smashing the ear, tearing the last sinews, and knocking the head into the air. As the head rolled into the street, the body dropped.

Nick found his gun and shot twice at the vampire carrying Jack. She landed on the roof. The were-bat followed. Nick shot twice more.

Every shot missed the vampire, or was useless, but he hit the were-bat in the small of the back. From his angle, that meant the bullet probably went up through the heart and exited near the throat. The bat crashed, hard, into the golem. Rats scattered. Blood rained from its wound.

The demon might have been the devil himself, except Nick always thought there'd be *two* horns and a pitch fork. It had a tail, yes, and a forked tongue. It hissed, having watching the vampire's leap, and vanished in a hot red cloud.

The golem slumped, already splattered and deformed, and began to melt. The rats dispersed into every available crevice. Neither the were-bat nor the walking corpse moved. Lisa managed to stand again.

Jack was gone.

7.

Lisa stared up the side of the building. She hadn't even seen the thing that grabbed Jack except as a blur.

A half dozen rat bites burned under her skin. Tears stung her eyes. She was muddy with clay. And helpless. "Can we follow it?" But she knew the answer. The coordinated attack had succeeded; Jack was already dead.

She wouldn't accept that, though.

She retrieved his bag, the laptop computer containing all his secrets. A database of the dark, of *evil*, of vampires and ghosts and — and maybe she could find something about the crimson behemoth who'd orchestrated the attack.

"We're not safe here," Nick said. She didn't even look at him. "We're being watched. Examined. They might attack again."

"Let them," Lisa said. It was a two-story brick building, a nightclub. She'd been on its roof just last week, dancing to a reggae band. The club might be locked, but she knew exactly where to find the stairs. "Open this door." She looked at Nick. Glared at him. Challenged him to say *No*. Instead, he shot the flimsy lock. The door shuddered, swinging inwards perhaps three inches. "There," he said.

She stormed through the door, into the pitch black of the club. She didn't look for the ghost. Didn't peer into shadows. She didn't care what else might lurk inside, didn't even look to see if the hunter followed.

In the very back of the club, past the bar and down the hall toward the bathrooms, absolute dark hid the staircase. She'd climbed them before, smiled prettily for the bouncer. Flirted. Followed Liz to dance under the moon. Not a spell, no ritual, no rite — just two women, among two hundred, looking for a good time.

The memories felt pale now, and thin.

The night hadn't been completely dark. Outside, ambient light spilled from everywhere, even the clouds. The moon had been visible for a while. There were streetlights, headlights, windows, signs.

Inside, there was nothing but the red exit sign.

The door at the top of the stairs was locked. Lisa twisted the knob, cursed, and kicked it. She shoved it with her shoulder, almost knocking herself back down the stairs. "You still with me, Nick?" she asked.

He said nothing, but gently moved past her. He knelt at the door, played with the lock a moment, then turned the knob.

It opened onto the roof.

8.

Jack Harlow's vision swam in and out of focus. They flitted over rooftops, jumping effortlessly from one to another, across alleys and streets, then to the higher buildings of downtown. Bank names shined from the peaks.

The rooftop around him was primarily gravel, tiny white rocks with concrete pavers leading from a door to the main air-handling unit, a metal storage shed, and various vents and grills.

The ascent had been dizzying. It was colder here. The wind blew more harshly. They stood on a two-foot-wide concrete ledge maybe six feet above the gravel rooftop — and over twenty stories above the street. Jack saw no details below. His eyes watered, blurring everything. He felt weak and cold.

He didn't quite know what had happened. He'd been stolen from the life he never got to live. His captor, if she chose, could just push him over the edge. She held him from behind, one arm curled under his shoulder and across his chest. Her hand was cold as the wind.

Waiting for death, Jack hoped for something quick and painless. Wished he could have been with Lisa instead, down on the street; how would she and Nick survive against that demon?

All thoughts fled when the vampire lowered her mouth to his neck. Warm lips — moist and soft. She licked from his collar bone to the base of his jaw, pausing to suckle, to drink the blood that had spilled from his wound. The were-bat had done that, hadn't it?

His head tilted back of its own accord — or *she* did it. He couldn't tell where his body ended and hers began. She must've supported him, because all strength vanished as her mouth moved across his throat — kissing, sucking gently, licking. His body trembled. Heat rose at his neck and spread.

Jack tried to lift his arm, to at least touch the hand that held him, but couldn't.

She slipped around his side, bending him backwards with the intensity of her kiss, one hand behind his spine and the other at the nape of his neck. As she drank, pulling blood from his wound, his senses faded — all but touch.

In a final burst of energy, he managed to reach behind her back. Tried to grasp her. Hold on. But when he tightened his fingers, his grip slipped, and then so did his consciousness.

If Jack Harlow dreamed, it was of the endless kiss of a vampire, and the bliss her victims felt in their final moments. Life slipped away effortlessly, without pain, without panic. In those last moments, when Jack existed only in his mind — where he expected to find eternal darkness — he instead felt a euphoria unsurpassed in human experience — complete and body-wracking and mind numbing.

The universe dissolved to her two lips on his throat, even in his dreams. With what he knew were his dying thoughts, he wished it was Lisa's kiss.

CHAPTER THIRTEEN

1.

Nick Hunter followed Lisa onto the rooftop.

The roof had been converted into a bar, as wide and deep as the downstairs, with a dance floor and colored lights, all dark, hanging on poles. Cheap but functional.

A stage stood in one corner, bathrooms to the side. There was a full bar behind a rolling, chain-link (and padlocked) fence. Rooftops to three sides were a matter of hopping four feet of bricks; the wall to the front was taller and overlooked the street.

There were plenty of places to hide, but Nick doubted the vampire used any of the nooks or false walls. She wasn't behind the wooden bar, nor on the other side of the shack-like bathroom set-up. The adjacent roofs were barren except for typical industrial vents and storage sheds; she wasn't there, either.

Lisa circled the outer edges of the rooftop. When she disappeared around the side of the stairs, Nick scanned the other rooftops.

Another long building was behind the club, as if they'd been built as twins, but it was empty and unused. Beyond it, past what was probably a road, were some trees and, not too distant, I-4.

To Nick's right, north, again there was only one building before the street. The store in the opposite corner was three stories high, so he couldn't see the roof. For a vampire with her demonstrated agility, that was not an impossible leap.

To his left, the rooftops continued, some higher or lower, with a dull regularity: one after the other, all the same, stretching maybe a hundred yards before ending abruptly. Across Orange Avenue, the climb was much higher, five stories.

"He's not here," Lisa said, coming again into view.

"No," Nick said, nodding to the north. "They went that way."

Lisa stared a moment. "Up there?" She pointed with her knife — Nick's knife.

He walked to the wall separating one roof from the other, seeing no sign of movement. "Not anymore."

Lisa nodded. Her eyes were steady, solid, teary but determined; otherwise, she was a mess of mud and blood. Her fists were clenched. She gripped the knife in her right hand so tightly her knuckles were white.

"You're a hunter," Lisa said, casting her eyes on him now. "Track them."

The vampire had gone downwind, so her scent would be carried away. Nick could make logical deductions as to which direction she might go from one roof to another. He had never tracked a specific beast before, and she hadn't made it easy.

He'd never seen one flee. She hadn't fled, exactly; she'd come down, taken her prey, and gone off to feast in private. It wasn't simply *rare*, it was unique in Nick's experience. They found corners, shadows, empty places where they could feed without interruption. The seductive type, like the vamp that took Jack, tended to troll clubs and bars, finding and luring away victims without spectacle.

Lisa waited for him to respond. Her eyes told him she'd hunt the beast alone, though she didn't know how — or what to do if she found it. Worse, if she found Jack already dead (probably the case), or a vampire himself now, she'd be dead (or undead) inside a minute — and she wouldn't care.

The moment he'd arrived, Nick had thought this city reeked of a vampire infestation. Now he realized he was wrong. It was much worse than that.

2.

Twelve hours ago, Lisa Sparrow would have laughed at the idea of fighting demonic armies. That was before teeth dropped out of the sky, before Jack unveiled the shadows. Her senses were open now, her night vision sharpened and her hearing more acute. She was fit. Ready and willing to fight for her love.

"We need to know more about what we've seen already," Nick said. "How to kill that red behemoth, for instance. And the clay thing, in case there's another."

The computer hung from her left hand, the straps of the soft briefcase crunched within her fist.

"And," Nick said, "we have to get away from here. Police will only slow us down." Until he said it, Lisa hadn't noticed the approaching sirens.

Lisa nodded. "We can't have that."

"This way," he said, going to the back of the club and scaling the four-foot brick wall.

They climbed down from the roof to an alley behind the club.

Lisa spent little time trying to puzzle anything out. It was useless to assert reason on anything she'd experienced tonight. She'd seen enough horror movies to know the constant skeptic died — horribly — crying at the end that she believed, truly believed, and needed no more convincing.

They moved more quickly now that they weren't the focal point of *every* shadow, past a clearing and under the I-4 overpass. Not so far they couldn't hear the police sirens or see flashing lights, but far enough so they could open the computer.

"It's almost morning," she said. The sky had brightened faintly.

"It *is* morning," Nick told her. "Newspapers have been delivered. Bakers have baked, bagel shops are hopping. Sunrise in...about twenty minutes."

"Vampires are night creatures, right?" Lisa asked. "I mean, the thing that took Jack, it won't be out during the day, will it?"

Nick hesitated. "*Most* sleep during the day, yes."

"So if Jack survives until sunrise," she said, though his chances seemed slim, "he'll probably be okay until sunset."

Nick didn't answer. He didn't have to. It was a false hope; he'd said *most*, not all, and his hesitation suggested *not this type*. And the other creature — the giant with bright red flesh — hadn't been vampires. They were subject to different rules.

3.

Nick Hunter opened Jack's database, spent a few minutes figuring out how to work it, and finally searched for vampires.

It listed eleven kinds. More than Nick had seen, but fewer than Chris Hunter had known about.

Nick scanned the pages of information, but it was mostly technical and overly detailed: temperatures, wind directions, dimensions of the rooms or alleys; the names of bars and bartenders; at least two victims' names and addresses. It lacked the information Nick needed: how to kill them, where they lived, weaknesses specific to their race of vampire.

He found a type of Chinese vampire: Chiang-Shih. It exhaled poison. When insubstantial, it became a sphere of light (like will-o'-the-wisps). Jack had apparently seen one in Chinatown (which Chinatown, it didn't say) half an hour before dawn. It was sitting in an alley, growling and hissing, counting grains of rice.

Nick found no particular name for the seductive vampire, and nothing he didn't already know. Fast, agile, strong, and devastatingly beautiful, they were mildly hypnotic and had a high level of pheromones.

"He saw her," Nick said.

"The vampire?"

"Just...a few nights ago, it looks like. Here. He talked to a ghost about her. No, the ghost talked to him. *Wanted to tell him stories.* This entry has both." Nick read more, summarizing for Lisa. "She winked at him. Touched his back."

Lisa had approached while he read and looked over his shoulder. "You sure it's the same one?"

"He describes her as Asian, dark hair to her shoulders, with brown, almost amber eyes." Nick shook his head. "Nothing else."

"Sounds like a lot of Asian women."

"Yes, but this is an Asian woman who also happens to be a vampire...a *western* vampire, not Asian, and at the same club. It's got to be her." Nick finished reading the brief entry. "It doesn't say anything else."

"How about how to kill it?" Lisa asked.

Nick opened his jacket, showing Lisa his silver and wood. "Got that covered."

"And the other thing?" Lisa asked. "With the red skin?"

Nick searched for *behemoth*, but found nothing. Red appeared all over the place, describing dozens of things — even the eyes of certain rats, which Nick had seen tonight. But for blister red skin, Nick found only one entry.

It described the place and the temperature (warmer around a gas station somewhere south of Route 80 in Pennsylvania, forty degrees elsewhere). A kid, working the night shift, had apparently read from some book (Jack hadn't named it) and summoned a nine-foot-tall mass of muscle in a cloud of reddish smoke. The creature grabbed the kid (and ignored Jack, who had stopped for a drink). The smoke thickened, and they vanished. Inside, Jack picked out his drink and a few things to eat. The creature's feet had left scorch marks in the cheap linoleum. Heat lingered. The counter had been burned.

Nick stared at the entry, at its title, unaware his mouth was hanging open until Lisa touched his arm. "What is it?"

"It," Nick said, swallowing hard, "is a full-fledged demon from Hell."

Lisa stared at the screen. "It doesn't say that."

"Demon." Nick pointed at the word. "It says *demon*. Where do you think they're from?" She didn't look as scared as Nick felt — which, oddly, reassured him.

She held his gaze. She had no tears any more, not even a hint of them. "Doesn't matter," she said. "We're going to kill it."

A moment of hesitation. Fear. All the things he didn't know, the knowledge and lore that existed outside his realm of experience, held him down. It wasn't too late to walk away; the watcher was gone, dead by now or a vampire himself.

But that was running away.

It wasn't Nick's fault she'd become involved in this, but he couldn't knowingly let Lisa hunt vampires without knowledge or preparation. He felt responsible.

But a *demon*.

Everything he knew about demons came from books or movies — and even there, his experience was slight. Ancient spells manifested demons, and spells sent them back. But Nick was no sorcerer. They'd met one earlier, the vaudoux, but Nick knew of no way to track a man who vanished at will.

Knowing this might be the last day of his life, Nick shut down the computer and inhaled deeply. "I think I know what we have to do. It's not the demon we need."

"It's the vampire," Lisa said.

Slowly, Nick shook his head. "No. The vaudoux."

They returned to the scene of the crime. There was no indication of it; the door had been shut, no police lingered outside the club, only smeared clay — like mud — on the wall.

Nick imagined the vaudoux was still nearby; he'd said he was "already close."

He went to the storefront where the witchdoctor had appeared, under a brown awning proclaiming "Best Sushi." The raw smoke smell lingered, heavily mixed with blood, sweat, and exhaust. The street was no longer empty; a few people walked the sidewalks, and cars and trucks lumbered down the one-way road.

"What, exactly, are we looking for?" Lisa asked. She knelt beside the door, touching the ground with one hand.

"He's got to be close," Nick said. "He appeared here, right before the attack."

"I don't think he attacked us."

"Then maybe he'll help," Nick said. "I've never fought a demon before. I don't know how they die. Or if."

"And the vampire?" Lisa asked. "You can track her, right?"

Nick looked skyward, to the rooftops across the street. "Won't do us much good if we find her just to die. Won't help Jack any, either."

Wherever he'd disappeared to, the vaudoux would have gone no further than line of sight. If he had summoned the demon, he must have been within sight of that, too, nearer the corner. Maybe it was as simple as summoning him. "Vaudoux," Nick said. "Show yourself."

CHAPTER FOURTEEN

1.

Lisa's belief system had to change. She'd grown up Catholic. Though she stopped attending church years ago — except for Christmas, because she enjoyed the choirs — she never stopped believing in God. The fundamental lessons she'd been taught as a child stayed with her.

There were ghosts and demons in the Bible, weren't there? She wasn't sure. Couldn't name one. People had been brought back from death — not just Jesus. Had Lazarus been like the zombie last night, without a mind, bound to another's commands? She didn't think so. There were variations; she'd learned that much already.

Jack was still alive. He had to be. She had some small amount of time left before the creatures did anything with him. The vampire could have slit his neck there and dropped Jack dead to the sidewalk, but that's not what happened. She took him. That had to mean something.

When Nick called the vaudoux, Lisa remained on one knee, fingers on the cold concrete. A shiver ran through her, fear and pain — not physical pain, but emotional, psychological, something deeper and more penetrating.

"Show yourself," Nick said again.

Lisa didn't believe the vaudoux had been responsible. It didn't feel right. The demon, the crimson-skinned giant, had directed the attack.

Wind gusted. The air warmed. The sky brightened while they waited. No one came. No puff of smoke, no smell of rotting flesh, no gnashing teeth, no vampire mistress, and no vaudoux.

"The demon," Lisa said.

Nick didn't stop her as she crossed the street, but didn't follow. He was scanning the rooftops as if he possessed x-ray vision that could penetrate the bricks.

Remnants of clay clung to the wall and sidewalk, but everything else was gone.

When she reached the spot where the demon had stood, heat struck her — it was ten, twenty, maybe thirty degrees hotter. Her breath caught and her vision swayed. Red smoke curled around her, soft and caressing, covering her ears and muting all sound. The sulfuric scent burnt her nostrils. The world flickered: bits of flame and smoke, swatches of shadow, the hard concrete under her feet. Her vision funneled, white creeping in from the edges, and the ground rose to meet her.

She threw out her hands. She felt nothing, but heard a distant cackling, a manic and ceaseless laughter, muffled as if underwater.

Maybe, at death, life passed before your eyes. Lisa saw only Jack, heard only his voice, smelled only his scent (which was what, exactly? Cinnamon musk? Essence of dark?), and felt only his touch.

Then concrete under her cheek, cold and unforgiving. Tentatively, she opened her eyes, afraid to find fire and smoke.

A hand on her shoulder, another under her head, lifted her cheek off the hard ground. A deep voice, low and barely audible, said a name — hers — and said it again.

At first, she saw only light and dark, then shades between. Focus came slowly, revealing Nick Hunter — not Jack — mouthing her name but sounding so far away.

She'd seen *something*. Her eyes burned with the vision.

"Lisa," Nick said again, sounding more human and real, as if he might actually be next to her.

"What happened?" Her words came out slurred and broken.

"You fainted," he said. "Fell. *You tell me* what happened."

"Hot," Lisa said. "I'm not sure, I can't say, it was...hot. Smoky. The demon, Nick...I heard it laughing."

"You saw it?" Nick asked, helping her sit up. The world swayed, but gently, nothing worse than the last time she'd drunk too much.

"Saw it," Lisa said, "and fire, and...it was like a cave, a big cave, with rivers of lava and men impaled on stalagmites, blood dripping from the ceiling...but I didn't see it, Nick, I didn't see anything at all."

"You only just fell," Nick said. "Weren't out for five seconds."

"It felt longer than forever."

"Jack," Nick said. "The vampire. Did you see them?"

Lisa concentrated, daring to recall the image she hadn't actually seen, this vision stuck in her mind like poison. It was like a snapshot, but the demon laughed. Smaller demons circled it — unimaginable beasts, horrid, twisted versions of reality, men and women chained to the walls by their hair, nails through their wrists, eye sockets empty. Souls stripped of flesh, muscles and sinews exposed, fought to escape the molten river, each pushing others down, each pushed down by others, and dog-like lion-ish things devouring any who reached the surface. Armies stood behind the demon, thousands and thousands assembled in formation, in a vast chamber filled with armored beasts and wicked blades that were like swords or axes.

Nick held her face, both cheeks, in warm hands. He was saying her name. Shaking her gently.

"No," she said, gripping Nick's wrist, unable to stop the tears. "No, Jack wasn't there. I didn't see Jack." She focused on Nick's eyes, never noticing before how blue they were — like powder, like dust. She locked her gaze there, afraid to slip into that other world, that hallucination. Nick's eyes were like the sky after noon, near evening but before dusk, flecked with snow, the eyes of a man who could be trusted and who meant what he said. A man driven, haunted, and tortured.

"Good," Nick finally said. "Then we only have to find the vampire. Can you stand?"

He helped her up. "I feel weak," she said.

"You need food," Nick said. "Then we find Jack."

2.

The diner was long and narrow, set between two shops. Barely past 6, the restaurant was already filled with people beginning their days, all bleary-eyed and clutching big mugs of coffee. Two frantic waitresses ran to and fro, one woman manned the counter, and a kitchen area in the back housed at least two cooks. Either nothing else nearby was open, or the food was good.

Nick led Lisa to one of the few open tables, then went to the counter to order them both fried eggs, toast and juice, and coffee for Lisa. They couldn't afford to waste the daylight; if she insisted on helping, she'd need to stay awake and alert.

He brought Lisa the coffee and juice. She wrapped her hands around the coffee cup. "Thanks."

"Food's coming," Nick said. "We'll have maybe eleven hours of daylight. Plenty of time to find Jack, if there's any trail."

Lisa sipped the coffee slowly. Deliberately. It slid down her throat and burned her stomach. No cream, no sugar; this was not the time. Other smells wafted around her: biscuits, cinnamon, eggs, grease. Fryers sizzled. Silverware clanked. Over everything, the smell of coffee was strong, and real, unlike anything she'd experienced overnight.

A number was called. "That's us," Nick said, getting up. Lisa opened her eyes and watched him approach the back counter. He passed a sea of unfamiliar faces. She was anonymous here, one of dozens or hundreds or thousands.

A woman sat in Nick's vacated chair and smiled. "I have something for you."

"Who are you?" Lisa asked.

The woman shrugged. "Like you, I'm looking for someone."

"What are you?"

"I'm...well, something like a witch. And I saw what happened. Your vision. I was out for a walk, no particular destination, and there you were." Her smile disappeared; she leaned closer, grabbing Lisa's hand. There was warmth there. "I think I'm close, but you're right there, so I want to help."

"How?" Lisa asked.

"My name's Sara," she said, holding out her other hand. She held a white bead. "I don't know if it'll help, but take it."

"What is it?" The crystal glowed. Pulsated.

"A bead of pure light," Sara said. "Never know when one might be useful." She set the bead next to Lisa's mug and stood.

"Wait," Lisa said. But Sara was walking toward the door before Nick returned. He gave Lisa an egg sandwich, had another for himself. "Eat fast," he said. "Clock's ticking."

They left the diner just like anyone else, through the front door, without a single head turning to see who or what walked amongst them. In this case, they were hunters; but other times, the secret dark things mingling with them might be worse.

Hunter. Lisa didn't like the designation, but it was apt. She'd become like Nick, not evil or dangerous, but bruised internally — and externally. The rest of the world was too absorbed by their own mundane lives — just as Lisa had been two days ago — to notice.

Outside, daylight filtered weakly through the clouds. The number of moving cars had doubled while they ate, and people walked everywhere.

"The clouds are a problem, aren't they?" Lisa asked.

"Only a little," Nick said, looking down the street. "The rain will be worse. Washes away scents."

"Scents?"

"Vampires reek," Nick said. "Putrid, like death, like rot. I can smell them."

They were walking, across the street from the club. Nick pointed at the rooftop. "I would've gone higher rather than lower. Get as far away as possible. So there." The club was near the corner; he pointed at the next building. "Then, maybe there." A row of four and five story office buildings. "Then, either up higher, or continuing northward, or angling back, away to the west."

Lisa stared for a moment. West of here, over the railroad tracks and across the interstate, was a residential neighborhood on the lower end of the economic scale. A lot of houses on their last legs were supported by concrete blocks. She avoided that district when she could, not interested in drugs or prostitutes, having no use for pawn shops, check cashers, or bail bondsmen.

North, the stores and shops eventually gave way to middle-class houses.

To go higher, the vampire couldn't have taken Jack far in any direction. Downtown was small, populated by maybe a dozen skyscrapers (or something like skyscrapers, infants compared to New York or Chicago's skyline).

Any of the three choices would be a lot of area to cover. "Which?" Lisa asked.

Nick shook his head.

"You're the hunter," Lisa said. "Where is a vampire like that likely to hide during the day?"

"Anywhere," Nick said. "But probably a cheap apartment. Motel. She wouldn't just find a hole and make it home. She'll actually live somewhere."

"Then office buildings are out," Lisa said. "This way." She never went there at night, rarely during the day, but she knew where to find cheap apartments and motels.

CHAPTER FIFTEEN

1.

It didn't take long.

Nick caught the scent shortly after crossing under the interstate. The walk had been uneventful; they passed a police station, parking lot, and railroad tracks before going beneath I-4.

Here, the streets thinned and the buildings grew more dilapidated. Roads and sidewalks were cracked, uneven, littered with random papers, plastic bags, and shattered glass. There were signs of cautious renovation.

They passed south of the arena and entered a residential district. There, near the burnt-out remains of a single-story apartment building, the deathly reek assaulted him.

A six-foot-high chain link fence protected the charred concrete. No wood had survived, and very little of the structure was lighter than charcoal. Three concrete buildings stood within the fence, all burned, with a sign: "Keep out, by order of the Orlando Fire Department."

"Fireman training," Nick said. "She's in there."

"You sure?"

Nick shook his head. "I can't say it's definitely *her*, but it is vampire."

Lisa inhaled deeply, loudly. "Yeah, I can smell it, too."

Nick pulled two stakes from his jacket and gave them to Lisa. "You'll need these," he said. "Most effective through the heart. I'll have to cut off her head after, but if you get the chance, pin her down."

A thick, heavy chain locked the gate. Nick scaled it easily, quickly, barely making a sound. He hopped down on the other side, drew his gun, and settled into his regular routine. He heard Lisa climbing behind him, but had already reached the doorway.

There was no door. The choice of such an open, exposed hideaway surprised Nick, but the scent was intense.

He entered gun first. He took in the front room quickly; there'd been no furniture when the place burned, or it had been cleared out. The ceiling was as charred as the walls and floor. He moved softly, slowly.

The front room was empty. There was a hallway, but Nick tried the one door first. It hid blistered remains of a bathroom. Some wallpaper clung to the wall in flakes. The toilet had been removed, leaving a hole and some pipes. The tub was cracked in the middle.

A mirror had hung over the missing sink. It had been shattered, either before or during the fire; pieces lay scattered on the floor, warped, more like a broken puddle than glass, black but still reflective.

He turned back to the front room. Lisa stood at the doorway, knife in one hand and stake in the other.

Nick slid against the wall soundlessly and entered the hallway low. Little light reached here, mostly through a hole in the ceiling. It led to two rooms on the right, a galley kitchen on the left.

Like the bathroom, the kitchen had been stripped to its pipes. The only cabinets were under the counter;

there were no doors on their skeletons, and nothing within.

Down the hall, he had to pick a room. Lisa stayed close behind; she moved more stealthily than he'd expected. He chose the leftmost room, sticking with his pattern. He entered low, gun first. Almost no light reached him here; the windows, though without glass, had been blocked by cardboard and plywood — after the fire.

He scanned quickly, his eyes enough adjusted to make out shapes and silhouettes within the shadows.

There.

Curled in the corner of the room like a baby, unmoving, sleeping like the dead. It wasn't the beast they were looking for. This was too pale, naked, hairless. It faced away from him as it slept. Nick slipped a stake from his jacket and advanced. Slow and cautious. It could still wake; daytime didn't leave them comatose.

He reached it, bent closer (always aiming the gun at its head, just in case), and plunged the stake into its back.

The thing shrieked. It shot up the side of the wall, crashed into the ceiling and fell back to the floor. It was hideous, its face deformed, eyes bulging, teeth sharp and crooked. With black oozing from its back, it reached for Nick.

He kicked the beast in the ribs and sent it back into the wall, driving the edge of the stake out through its chest.

"Knife," Nick said, but Lisa wasn't there.

2.

Lisa never followed Nick into the room. She had no grandiose ideas of exploring the other room on her own. Fit as she was, she had never trained with a knife. She didn't know how she'd react if she stabbed something and its blood spilled over her — warm or cold.

So she watched Nick approach the vampire and, holding her breath, gripped the knife. When he staked it, the creature leapt, smashing the ceiling, knocking dust and ash from it. It squealed — and so, too, did something in the room behind Lisa.

There'd been two rooms at the end of the hall. Lisa stepped away from the two doorways.

"Knife," Nick said. Calmly. Quietly. He hadn't heard the other creature.

It shot through the hall, running straight across from the one room to the other, either ignoring or unaware of Lisa shaking in the hallway. It screeched a vicious, ear-piercing sound of fury. This was female, naked and sickly white, hairless like the other, arms swinging wildly.

Lisa followed it in, hoping there wasn't a third. It leapt at Nick. He sidestepped, knocked it forward, but lost his gun in the same motion. The creature's claws slashed down, maybe drawing blood. It was too dark for Lisa to be sure.

The thing spun quickly, attacking with both claws, face contorted with rage, spitting and hissing. Nick fell back, catching its hands, kicking with one leg as he rolled onto his back. He threw the creature over him; it crashed into the wall at Lisa's right.

She swung the stake and knife together, burying both in the vampire's chest and gut. It squealed, wriggled, lashed out. It smacked Lisa, throwing her into the doorjamb.

Then Nick rushed forward. He yanked the knife free and slashed its throat. Thick fluid, black in the dark, spit out of its neck. Nick drove the knife deeper, severing the head.

The creature's body slumped. Before Nick could turn, the first vampire, stake still protruding from its chest, grabbed him in a bear hug and rolled backwards to the floor. Nick cried out in pain; the beast screamed. They rolled toward the window.

Lisa scrambled forward, finding Nick's fallen pistol. She'd never shot a gun in her life. It was heavy in her hands, both hot and cold.

Nick was on top, but on his back. The creature squeezed, and its mouth went for his neck. Nick wrenched himself forward, breaking its grip long enough to roll away.

Lisa fired, point blank, into the vampire's face. It exploded in a spray of bone and brain. Teeth scattered on the floor.

The sound was deafening. The force of the gun threw Lisa's hand up and back; she was surprised to have hit it, even from less than a yard away. The creature slumped, arms flailing in the spot its head had occupied, then dropped.

For a moment, the room was still. Both vampires were dead, or re-dead. Lisa lowered the pistol. Its acrid smell filled the room. Her arm burned, her face stung, her back ached, her ears rang.

Lisa hesitated. She'd never killed anything, never fought for her life before — or someone else's life. She didn't enjoy it, no, but she felt just a little more powerful. She *could* do it. If she had to.

But these vampires were nothing like the one that had snatched her lover.

Nick managed to get to his hands and knees; Lisa helped him the rest of the way up. He swayed, relying on her for support, and staggered toward the fallen vampires.

"Not done." He withdrew a heavy duty lighter from an interior pocket in his jacket and shrugged free of Lisa's hold. He moved slowly, wincing as he knelt next to the nearest vampire. He ignited the lighter, and lowered the flame to the pulpy remains of its head.

Fire flashed through its body, brightening the room. Thick smoke rose, but briefly; the fire was out as soon as it started. The new burnt odor was barely noticeable over the old.

In the same manner, Nick destroyed the second vampire.

Lisa closed her eyes. The more she saw, the less afraid she was of seeing the demon inside her eyelids. The hellish realm remained strong, but she knew now she wouldn't slip helplessly to it every time she rested. She shook all over. Anxiety, fear, exhilaration, it was hard to pinpoint why.

"That," Nick said, grinning, "was fun."

"You're a mess," she told him.

"I'm hiding it well."

"This was the wrong place."

He didn't answer. She opened her eyes again, glanced around the room, wishing this had ended. Hadn't that been tough enough, without having to do an encore when they found Jack? How many creatures would they have to fight their way through to get to him? This wasn't a video game. There were no levels, each harder than the last, leading to the ultimate bad guy. Eliminating these two brought them no closer to their goal.

Nick removed his shirt, revealing muscles she hadn't quite expected, and tried to look over his shoulder and down his back. "I was hit."

Lisa stepped closer, looking at the round wound half way down his back.

"Is it a scratch?" he asked. "Bite?"

"Neither, I don't think."

Nick sighed, relieved, and pulled his shirt back on. "Stabbed?"

"Maybe," Lisa said. "I'm not an expert."

"I think it got me with my own stake. It was sticking out of its chest when it grabbed me. I'm lucky."

"Lucky?" Lisa asked.

"If it had been a bite, you would have to kill me. A scratch, I *might* be okay." Nick paused. "They didn't get you, did they?"

"She slapped me."

"Break the skin?" Nick asked.

"No."

"Good."

After a moment's silence, Lisa asked, "Is it always like this?"

Nick didn't answer. Instead, he retrieved the stakes from the ground and returned them to his jacket. Then he held out his hand for the gun.

Lisa gave it to him. Her arm felt enormously lighter, but empty and weak.

"Still want to search?" Nick asked.

"Damn right, I do."

"Good. This may be a long day."

3.

Nick Hunter hurt.

He wouldn't let Lisa know quite how much, but he was lucky the stake hadn't done any real damage. The pain stretched in every direction — across his skin, up his spine, and into his gut. Every step hurt.

Under normal circumstances, with a wound like this, he'd find a motel room, sleep for a day, and swallow painkillers for breakfast. But he was on a mission now. He didn't quite understand how he'd gotten drawn into it, but he liked having a goal more specific than *kill another beast*. It made him feel useful. Necessary. He missed having a partner.

He liked Lisa. She was a hunter, regardless of what she'd been before. He'd have to train her, teach her, show her things. They'd have to trust each other intrinsically if they planned to make a habit of this. She was fit, and fearless, and she'd seen things Nick had never seen. Lisa would make a good partner.

One step at a time, Nick walked, staggered, or swayed. The pain lessened. He concentrated, instead, on the destination. The quest. Neither hope nor fear had been part of his life, not since Diane died; but now he felt a little of both.

They checked the other two structures. Both were just as burned out, torn apart inside and out, but there were no other beasts.

The charred smell lingered in his nostrils. He had to get rid of it. He also had to wash.

Lisa waited outside while he broke into the bathroom on the side of a gas station. The station itself shut down and abandoned, its windows boarded and signs smashed. No one had touched it for months. Two restrooms were around the side. He hoped water still ran through the pipes, but would have been satisfied with enough paper towels or toilet tissue to wipe away most of the gunk.

Water trickled out of the faucet. No pressure, but he cupped his hands underneath and cleared his face. After wringing out his shirt, he examined his wound in the mirror.

It didn't look as bad as it felt, barely more than a pinhole. He washed it and tested its depth. His whole fingernail went in, sending ripples of pain as far as the nape of his neck. Okay, it was worse than it looked — deeper, anyhow.

He rinsed himself as best he could, drying with crumpled newspaper. He moved slowly, giving his pain some time to subside. It would slow him down, and that could be deadly.

He pushed out of the bathroom. "Your turn."

Lisa screwed her face, apparently dreading the thought, but went inside anyway.

4.

The rain started as a sprinkle.

Lightning cracked the sky. The rain intensified, even as Lisa Sparrow emerged from the restroom station. Thunder crashed.

CHAPTER SIXTEEN

1.

First, he heard thunder.

Slowly, Jack Harlow opened his eyes. His throat was sore, his head groggy, his vision blurry. He rubbed his neck, trying to figure out what he was looking at. The city stretched below him — far below. He was at the edge of a window, in no danger of falling, seated in a rather comfortable leather chair. He was in an office.

He spun the chair slowly to see the rest of the room. Besides the window and the chair, there was only a heavy wood desk. Fluorescent lights, dark, hung low from the ceiling. All light came from outside and didn't amount to much.

The carpet was flat and blue, the walls gray, the chair black, and the door closed. He didn't know where he was, and couldn't even be sure he was still in Orlando. He didn't know it well, but he could see lakes, trees, and other buildings through the window which seemed right.

He was neither bound nor dead. The last thing he remembered was a kiss...no, a bite...a lick? A dull ache throbbed behind his eyes.

Outside, it was daytime but stormy. He'd survived the night. She'd neither killed nor turned him.

Rain splattered the window. He was thirsty. Before Jack could gather the strength to stand, the office door opened. The hall behind was dark, as well. The vampire stepped out of those shadows carrying a Styrofoam cup.

"You're awake."

"I know you." Jack squinted, still not able to see clearly. Petite, with short black hair, Asian eyes and skin — he'd seen her the other night in the club.

"We've met, yes," she said. "I'm Jia Li." She set the cup on the desk, then jumped up there herself. She crouched so she didn't tower over him, but looked down nonetheless.

She was beautiful. Stunningly beautiful. Her eyes cinched it: so light a brown they were almost amber, with yellow eye shadow making a thin mask that stretched to both sides and accentuated the already narrow, almond shape. She smiled, her lips a shade darker than her skin. She showed a lot of skin under form-fitting black. Of course, she was a particular type of vampire — designed to seduce every sense.

"How's your neck?" she asked.

"Sore." Jack felt no bite marks, not even the slash of the were-bat's claws.

"It ought to be," she said. "It had been torn open when I found you." She smiled. With one hand on the desk in front of her, she looked like a cat ready to pounce. Every muscle in her legs and arms were tight, and the dress revealed everything. "I really couldn't resist," she said. "I had to taste you. I needed it."

"Needed?"

"It's like sex," Jia Li said. She spoke slowly, softly. "Drinking is very intimate, and sometimes disappointing. But you...you were extraordinarily satisfying." She licked her upper lip. "I'm very particular when I choose a partner."

"Victim," Jack corrected.

She shook her head once, touched his lips with her warm finger. "Partner," she said again, "though somewhat more like the black widow, I suppose. I've never heard a complaint."

She was close, painfully close; a wild, exciting scent drifted from her skin, and even her breath. Her finger lingered on his mouth. It quickened Jack's heart. "But if you died," she said, "I couldn't enjoy you again. And I want very much to taste all of you." She slid her hand across his cheek and behind his neck, pulling his face toward hers. "Oh, I admit, there's a strong urge to snap your neck, rip open your throat, gorge myself in a short-lived orgy. But I'm a patient girl. And lonely."

She kissed him, lightly, on the lips, with a soft lust. Every fiber of Jack responded, though he didn't move. His mind jumbled. He tried to focus on something else, someone else. He was too weak.

"I hope you never die," Jia Li said. "I'll kill for you, lover. To have you even as a human woman might. To know you like you've never been known. Eternity is not mine to give. But for as long as you last, I will savor every delectable minute."

Jack tried to move, but couldn't even look away from her.

"Do you know what it's like, to be a god?" Jia Li asked. "To walk among humanity for a thousand years, never aging, never tiring, never growing weak?"

"The sun," Jack said.

She smiled. Gorgeously. "Overrated."

"Vampires die," Jack said.

"At the hands of your hunter? Your girlfriend?" Jia Li asked, chuckling. "I am not worried. And don't you fret, either, love, we are safe here. Protected."

"From what?"

"You have walked the dark all your short life," Jia Li said. "You know what's out there, or at least a small part of it. You've witnessed, first-hand, things that most would die for seeing. This, I think, is what makes you so wonderfully delicious. And the electricity, when I touched you that first time, in the bar, when I knew I couldn't have you." She shuddered. "You left me breathless. And now, I can share everything with you, give you all I am, until you can take no more." She raised an eyebrow. "And then, you will give me all you are, all you have, until you're drained of every fluid and every ounce of strength, until you cannot even open your eyes. Then you'll sleep. Rest. Recover. And we can do it all over again."

"I have nothing to give you," Jack said.

Jia Li laughed. She shifted her weight back, still balanced on the desk, and looked down at the cup. "Drink," she said. "You need water."

It looked like a regular, ordinary cup you might find in any office kitchen.

"I'm not going to poison you," Jia Li said.

The water was cold, refreshing. He drank it in two gulps, then dropped the cup on the floor; he didn't have the strength to return it to the desk.

"I have had many lovers," Jia Li said, "but few in the style in which you're familiar. Like I said, the drink is orgasmic. I have to be careful not to lose myself with you; I am not indestructible. I can forget myself. And right now, with you, I have never been in more danger of losing my senses. *Never.* You're like no other lover I've had." She leaned forward again, whispering. "Why do you think I want to keep you?"

Jack inhaled deeply, trying to find energy in the air. "I won't be willing."

"No?" Jia Li kissed him again, warm and wet. Her tongue slid gently across his lips, then between them. She held his head in one hand; he could not resist. It was heavenly. Mind-numbing. His whole body craved this kiss.

He tried to focus on Lisa, but through clouded thoughts.

Lightning played across the sky outside. Thunder rumbled. Rain poured. Jia Li's kiss continued. She drew his tongue into her own mouth, caressing it with her teeth. Jack had no will anymore.

Jia Li pulled away even as Jack strained forward. She held his head, though, and kept his mouth an inch from her own. "Are you willing now?" she whispered. "I really want you to stay with me as long as you can. I'm just afraid you don't have much time left."

Jack couldn't see straight, and could barely put two thoughts together. It was hard enough to react to what was happening, and he was failing that. He managed to grasp this thread. "What do you mean, not much time?"

Jia Li shrugged. "You're the watcher, you tell me. Those things in the street, the demon and were-bat...I've seen all those before, don't look so surprised. It takes a powerful demon to direct that much at once. And the rats, did you see them? I hate rats."

"You're a vampire," Jack told her.

"I'm a girl," she said. "A child, to some, but old enough..." Her grin broadened. "It's past dawn, and it may have been your last. I imagine whatever you did to get that demon after you, he won't give up because I got you first."

"I did nothing," Jack said. "Never saw it before tonight."

"This morning," Jia Li corrected him. "Doesn't matter, you're attracting things. Just look around. There's a reason I took you here instead of home. I have a great view of the city — half the city from this window alone. I keep these offices for a number of reasons. I never thought I'd need them as a stronghold."

"Stronghold?" Jack asked.

"It'll be a long time before the rats can climb twenty-seven stories," she said. "Same with the roaches. They keep this building pretty clean. Anything else, I'll see it coming."

"You mean to keep me," Jack said.

"Exactly," Jia Li said. "If I must fight for you, I will. But a demon...those are big, you know. Nasty. Not exactly going to turn and run when I go *Boo.*"

"You'd risk your own life?"

"You're unique," Jia Li told him, though he wasn't sure if she said it or if he dreamt it. "You're a power." She narrowed her eyes, intensifying the effect of the make-up mask around them. "I absolutely *love* power."

2.

The storm raged — hard rains and icy wind. Clouds hid the sun so well it might as well have been midnight.

Dark cloaked the city. The weathermen said conditions were ripe for tornados. Expect the rain to continue into Saturday. Possible flooding. Stay home, they warned, if you can. Stay dry.

3.

The search felt long, endless, and excruciatingly slow.

By noon, Lisa Sparrow's legs ached. That was hours ago. Constant rain had pruned her skin. She shivered, but followed Nick through abandoned homes and ruinous motels.

The streets were mostly empty of pedestrians, and people driving by didn't bother about two strangers wandering their neighborhood.

Every time she thought of Jack, Lisa felt a stab of rejuvenation, as if simply invoking his name made up for the lack of sleep, hours of walking, and the pitiless rain.

Lightning crashed all around them.

Their pattern had taken them west first, then north, where they crisscrossed every road and alleyway. Residents stared, but from windows and doorways. The rain washed away whatever blood and gunk they hadn't rinsed off in the gas station. Finally, they found themselves back on Orange Avenue, maybe two miles from where they'd started.

"They could be in another state by now," Lisa said.

"Could be," Nick said, "but vampires are territorial. A few square miles, at the most."

Lisa imagined walking in the rain with Jack, maybe alongside Lake Eola, hands together, breeze at their backs, the fountain glowing and a sliver of moon shining. But the scene shifted, the water reddened and thickened. The sky became rock, and then the ground, and walls formed behind her.

Jagged lightning broke through the unreal image, becoming part of it. The demon laughed, and souls in agony cried and screamed and clawed at each other.

Then the vampire swooped down, snatching Jack again, yanking his hand from Lisa's and leaping into the lake that had become molten rock. The vampire bounced from one head to another, carrying Jack under one arm. The souls she trod over reached for her, but always too late. The demon stopped laughing. But the vampire and Jack weren't really there; only Lisa was, and the demon, and its horde...

Lisa still felt the heat when she dragged herself free, back to the street and rain. Asphalt, concrete, glass, steel, trees, clouds...none of these things existed in the demon's mirage.

Nick stared at her.

"I keep slipping," she said.

He squeezed her hand. "We'll find him."

Yeah, she wanted to say, but then what? Every time she slipped, it became more real, more solid. The heat increased, and she almost felt the demon's breath.

Before beginning another sweep of another street, Nick said, "We're doing this wrong."

4.

Jack Harlow drifted in and out of dreams. Jia Li seemed to leave him alone, though he twice woke to stabs of pain — once in his neck, once his wrist. He didn't know what was real, what was imagined, what was forced upon him.

Jia Li often perched on the desk. Sometimes she seemed to watch him, tilting her head to one side or narrowing her eyes. Other times, she faced away from him. She wasn't always there. When Jack wanted water, the cup was always full and sometimes cool.

Once, he saw something else — perhaps a phantom — also staring at him. Jia Li either didn't notice or didn't care.

Noise from the next room woke him once; the crashing continued until a final bang shook the wall. Dust fell from the ceiling tiles. A dull thud followed, and then silence — except for the storm.

Sometimes, Jack thought he was in the grip of night. Lightning flashed like strobes, contrasting the shadows. He saw everything as if he watched low quality black and white video on a cheap television. Nothing was clear — except Jia Li; when she was there; he saw her perfectly.

Finally, he woke. For real.

Jia Li, on the desk, smiled. "Feeling any stronger?"

"No," Jack lied.

Her grin faltered. "This storm blurs the line between day and night. Won't be long before the sun doesn't matter."

"Is that why we're still here?" Jack asked.

"We're here," Jia Li said, "because this is my nest. My aerie, you might say. I can see miles in every direction. There is no place safer."

"But I'm still going to die," Jack said.

Jia Li shrugged. "Life is one long death. From the moment you are born."

"Even for you?" Jack asked.

She smiled.

"Tell me something."

She leaned close, licking her top lip, and whispered. "Anything."

"What happened? What changed?"

"Honestly," Jia Li said, "and I have no desire to be anything but honest, I don't know and I don't care. When I saw you the other night, so confident and quiet, with those wonderful chocolate eyes drinking me and drowning me, you were off-limits. When I touched you, barely a brush, I felt it on a cellular level. Physically, I responded. It was dangerous. More contact might have killed me, but the pleasure was worth it. We were like magnets, repelling each other, but I wanted more. I don't know how else to describe it. You had an electricity."

"No longer?" Jack asked.

"Oh, it's there." Jia Li placed her palm on his cheek. "An undercurrent, stronger and more vibrant than before. Do you not feel it, through my hand?"

Jack nodded. He did feel it, something akin to static electricity.

She climbed down from the desk, straddled him — legs on either side of the chair — and settled into his lap. "It's why I find you so irresistible."

"I was untouchable."

She kissed him, and again, light pecks on both sides of his mouth. "*Was*, yes. Past tense."

"But you say it's still there."

"Oh, yes." Jia Li's eyes riveted his gaze, paralyzing him. "But it flows...differently." She kissed him, lingering. "Makes you very, very touchable. And your lips so kissable, and your throat..." She yanked Jack's head back by his hair, exposing his neck, pushing the chair back as she did so. "I have never tasted a man so luscious." She made a soft, slow trail of kisses up his throat. He heard his heartbeat — or was it hers? No teeth, just lips and tongue, and every subtle curve of her body melted into him.

He couldn't resist. Didn't want to. She overwhelmed every sense. He lifted his hands to her hips. Slipped one around to the

small of her back, the other down her thigh. Solid but yielding. He felt the muscles under her skin.

Internally, Jack struggled not to lose himself. He was not supposed to be a vampire's plaything. He'd found true love, something more powerful than he understood. Nothing Jia Li did could chase Lisa Sparrow from his heart. But when the vampire came close, his mind scrambled. Thoughts failed to connect. Memories scattered.

She reached between them to undo his jeans, her voice breathy and quiet now. "I can barely remember the last time I had a man like this." She unbuttoned enough to release him.

For a moment, Jack felt absurdly exposed. A twinge of fear, rational and very real, opened his eyes. This wasn't something he wanted to do, but he absolutely had no will to resist.

Jia Li drew breath through clenched teeth as she slid down onto him — unhurried — gently — *what fear?* They sighed in unison. She moved very slowly, savoring every sensation, luxuriating in it, as if time had stopped, and the world had ended, and the universe had been reduced to two inextricable bodies making love in the erratic light of exploding thunderbolts.

CHAPTER SEVENTEEN

1.

The storm made tracking by scent impossible. However, the storm helped direct them. The wind, like every other creature of the night, was drawn to the watcher. If he had just relaxed and let instinct take over, Nick might have followed the same force.

Lisa hurried to keep up. "What happened?"

"The wind," Nick said. "It led me to Jack once." He didn't know how to explain it. There had been other signs, last night, and looking around now revealed nothing to justify his sudden certainty.

Huddled against the door of a former clothing store (sign still etched on the window, but nothing visible inside except empty racks), a vagrant clung to his brown-bagged bottle. Wine, whiskey, whatever. He sipped absently, his vacant eyes more or less watching the sky — not just any section of sky, but the very direction Nick was headed.

"Don't," the vagrant said.

Nick stopped and looked again. The vagrant was a bundle of rags, layers of variegated colors, all worn to dull gray and brown and black. Fingerless gloves and a disintegrating wool cap. He'd managed to stand, leaving the bottle tucked in the corner of his alcove. He steadied himself with the door and stumbled into the rain pointing a thick, dirty finger at Nick and Lisa. "Don't."

"Don't what?" Lisa asked.

The vagrant shook his head. "It's all over," he said, his voice rough but sad. "All of it, over, done. I'll miss it."

"Miss what?"

The vagrant squinted at her and scratched the side of his scraggly beard. "All of it."

Nick grabbed Lisa by the arm. "Let's go."

They got one step before the vagrant raised his voice. "Hear me! Heed me! I am no mere fool who has drunk himself into oblivion! I have seen things that would make grown men weep in fear."

"Another watcher?" Lisa whispered.

Nick shook his head. "I don't think so."

"I was a lieutenant," the vagrant said, his volume back to normal. "I led the army over the hill. I took his head myself."

Nick hesitated.

"It's still dark," the vagrant said, "night or no, and we shall not be put down again!" He rushed forward, arms outstretched.

Nick deflected the attack, letting the vagrant fall forward — almost into the street. The vagrant spun, drool hanging from his oversized mouth, sharp teeth suddenly visible, and also the gaps where they had rotted away. The whites of his eyes were yellow, huge now, intent on Nick. He attacked again.

Nick caught the vagrant's arm between his fists (one at the wrist, one at the elbow). It cracked — loudly. The vagrant screamed, enraged; his broken arm fell limp, but he lunged again.

This time, the vagrant feigned his attack; Nick blocked air, and the vagrant struck his chest. Brown and cracked fingernails extended, like claws. Nick fell back, knocking Lisa aside.

"I was the second lieutenant," the bum said, lowering his head, "and I will miss all of it."

Then he burned.

It wasn't like lighting a vampiric flash. Flames rose from the vagrant's arms, his legs, his gaping mouth. His eyes blazed. The woolen hat flaked away as his head burst into flame. He stumbled to one knee, laughing, and turned his attention toward Lisa. "I will miss you most of all."

Then he fell — and continued to burn.

2.

Like her dreams, Lisa's visions had been neither memories nor imagination; every time she saw the demon's realm, the lava rivers and the tortured souls, she entered a real place, if only in her mind.

She'd taken an extra moment to watch the vagrant fall because he wasn't typical: not a man like other streetwalkers, but not a demon. A hybrid. A failure. He'd been cast from his home, but Lisa saw echoes of the demon's realm in his eyes. Now, Lisa feared for her life. After saving Jack, they had to find a way to save her.

The demon glared at her through the hybrid's eyes. This, at least, was just a remnant of memory, the last he'd seen before being abandoned on earth. The demon had armies behind him. *Legions.*

Lisa didn't *know* any of this; it was assumption and conjecture. Her crash course in the ways of darkness neared an end; she couldn't guess the final outcome. The demon had been intent on Jack, but what if its target had changed?

After the first step away from the hybrid, she was jogging. Two or three yards later, she broke into a run.

She glanced back as she ran. Nick tried to catch her, but he didn't run like she did — every day, morning and night, three or five miles, sometimes ten. She'd run marathons.

Thick smoke rose from the lieutenant, within which a rift opened. The small crack closed when the fire abruptly went out — but not before something slipped through, something no bigger than a man, winged and dark, camouflaged by the smoke and a sudden conflagration of lightning fracturing the sky over the hybrid's body.

Lisa slowed to a stop and waited for Nick. There was no point in running. No point in hiding. Something — a scout or soldier — had come through from the demon's realm.

3.

The fire had died, but the smoldering corpse emitted plumes of smoke. Lisa's eyes, however, seemed focused not on the burnt thing on the sidewalk, but above it. High above it.

Nick saw nothing, even when lightning momentarily lit everything. The smoke looked like an alien landscape, cloud-like mounds of ever-changing black, as if the air itself had been charred.

"Come on," Nick said, trying to push Lisa further away.

"Yeah," she said. "Let's go."

Then she flickered — like a red spotlight slid over her, glimmering from one side of her body to the other.

Nick stopped and blinked.

"What?"

"You..." Nick hesitated. "Did you just see it again? The demon, I mean?"

Lisa closed her eyes. Otherwise, she didn't move. The scarlet glimmer crossed her again. Twinkled. It corresponded with a blaze of lightning, a crack of thunder, and the unearthly cry of an airborne beast.

Nick looked. It reminded him of the batboy, but this thing had dark green skin, scales perhaps, talons and wide wings. It was visible for only a moment before it slid above the clouds.

"*The first lieutenant,*" Lisa said. She shuddered. The whites in her eyes shifted to crimson, then black. She doubled over, retching, grasping Nick's arm.

"We've got to get you some help."

"There is no help," Lisa said. The scarlet gleam came again, passing also through Nick's arm, tips of his fingers to his shoulder blade, then spread through his entire body like pins and needles.

A world of rock. Stone. Stalactites and stalagmites like teeth. A molten river. Two beasts, yoked like oxen, dragged a cage, but they weren't animals. They were men and women conjoined and twisted, heads where feet should be and behind the neck and along the side — bodies melted haphazardly together. In the cage, thin and pale people with featureless faces screamed mouthlessly and reached for him through the slats of the prison wagon.

The expanse stretched infinitely despite the cavernous walls. There were hundreds of variations. Thousands. Many lined up like soldiers. Winged beasts flew overhead. Smaller things clung to every available surface, hiding behind each other, fighting for deeper, safer refuges; and even smaller things, like spiders, crawled over them.

At the center of it all: the demon. The same red behemoth that had been on the street, but bigger, broader. Laughing as it came closer, its every step rocked the ground. Creatures scurried in all directions and cowered.

Lisa still clutched Nick's arm.

"You," the demon said, its heavily browed eyes meeting Nick's gaze. "I do not want." The demon shoved the air. The concussive force struck Nick full in the chest and knocked him backwards, out of Lisa's grip, back onto the street alone.

4.

The world flickered, as if the film of Lisa's life had jumped off the spool.

Then they *were* here, solidly, no longer just an image in her mind. Then Nick was gone, leaving her alone with the demon — and the millions of smaller things scattered around them. While everything else fled, the strength oozed from Lisa's legs as if her feet melted into the ground.

Flames erupted from the nearby magma river as something dove into it.

With Nick gone, the demon turned to Lisa. "You, however." He stopped directly in front of her, no longer laughing. She heard the silence now; even the scurrying quieted, as if every little creature feared the demon's attention.

"Me?" she asked, trying not to betray her terror. Courage was not the *lack* of fear, but the ability to face it. Presently, she stood before the unearthly embodiment of horror. Jack's computer, still in her hands, was no weapon.

The demon looked down at her; he stood nearly twice her height. "We have much to discuss."

5.

"No," Nick protested, but he spoke to no one. Smoke danced into the sky like a snake escaping the self-immolated corpse. A series of thunderbolts rumbled, near and far, creating a single, undulating sound. The wind grew fierce. The rain intensified. Police approached the burnt vagrant.

He wanted to go after Lisa. But how? He couldn't go the way she'd gone. The second lieutenant would give no answers. The winged monstrosity that had climbed into the clouds? Nick didn't know its scent or sound.

He glanced at his watch. Damn. He'd lost twenty minutes. Less than two hours till sunset — not that he'd be able to tell. If anything, the storm intensified.

He didn't consider himself a hero. He did what he had to, messy though it may be. But now he felt connected, damn them. He had to see this through to the end.

CHAPTER EIGHTEEN

1.

Jack Harlow had never felt so weak — physically, mentally, or emotionally.

Jia Li had pulled her skirt back down and left, returning only to bring fresh water. She hadn't taken blood, but still left him drained. At least he was consciousness now, and able to keep his eyes open. He shifted the chair so he could see both the front door and out the window with just a turn of his head.

It looked like Armageddon out there: roiling clouds and lightning tendrils. Deep, penetrating dark shrouded everything. Above those clouds, day hadn't ended yet.

But dusk was near, and the light low; the earliest of the night creatures were rising.

There were eyes out there. They'd watched him all last night and would watch again tonight. A wolfish man perched on a rooftop far below, his maw stretched wide to drink the rain. Shadows shifted. Jack rarely saw the rooftops; he was used to the undersides, and never realized so much existed so high. A gargoyle ripped free from the top of a church and glided away. A brigade of rats marched on a rooftop across the street. They continually glanced up at Jack's window.

Despite the electricity flowing so freely in the air, things flew: two or three types of demon; a few huge birds — *rukhs*, though Jack knew they shouldn't have been here; a warrior woman on a horse? Jack blinked, certain he hadn't actually seen a Valkyrie. Was a hero about to fall, or was she simply attracted by the same force that brought everything else? He even caught a glimpse of a flying snake, which could not be as large as he imagined and could not possibly be a *dragon*.

Faces formed in the clouds, in the shadows, in the rain itself circling Jia Li's aerie.

Flies landed on the window, only to be washed away by the rain. A lizard, no more than four inches long, had managed to scale the entire building and clung to the window a few feet to Jack's left.

In the glass, Jack saw his own reflection. Ashen. Dark splotches under his eyes. He saw two of himself, first thinking it was a trick of his vision, then maybe the window itself. But his doubled reflection was real. Substantial. And directly behind him.

Jack drew upon every ounce of strength and willpower to reach behind him for the double. He caught it by the neck before it could move and yanked it forward — or tried. Jack managed only to pull himself backwards and swivel the chair.

The movement brought him face to face with his doppelganger. One hand around its neck, the other gripping its shoulder.

"What do you want with me?" Jack asked.

The doppelganger was more ethereal than Jack, translucent and feather-light, but otherwise identical. It even wore the same clothes. "*Ich verstehe dich nicht.*"

Jack shook it, wrapping both hands around its neck. "I'm tired of this."

In fact, Jack was well beyond tired. He couldn't keep his hold on the doppelganger. It slipped his grip, turned, and ran. It got as far as the door, where it rebounded off

Jia Li. It toppled backwards, stunned. The vampire didn't budge, but looked down. "What's this?"

"Doppel…"

She shot Jack a vicious look then, with one hand around its throat, bent at the knees and lifted it off its feet. It swung its legs uselessly, gripped her hand. Flailing both arms, it struck Jia Li again and again without effect.

She pulled its face closer to her mouth. "Looks like you."

"*Nein.*"

Smoothly, Jia Li lowered her mouth to its throat and drank.

Jack felt a rush of jealousy — also excitement — an unadulterated, inescapable physical need.

The doppelganger moaned and sighed. Tension fled visibly from its muscles until it slumped in Jia Li's arms. She tossed it aside.

Licking a drop of blood from the corner of her mouth, she said, "Doesn't taste nearly so sweet as you."

2.

"That was a doppelganger," Jack said.

Jia Li tilted her head, then looked at the corpse she'd casually tossed away.

"Means I'm going to die," Jack said.

"You don't understand your own mythologies, do you?" Jia Li asked. "You think the stories that survive today are exact replicas of the original tales, based on actual events and creatures. When you say vampire, you think I cannot walk in churches, garlic scares me, I sleep in a bed of earth." Casually, she strolled toward Jack, put a hand on either armrest, and lowered her face to his. "In fact, I love the architecture in many churches. And the taste of garlic. The bed on which I sleep..." She kissed the corner of Jack's mouth. "Satin sheets. I love all things sensual. Sure, it's a boring stereotype, but not the one you expected, is it?"

"There are other vampires," Jack told her, "whose strength fails in daylight. But the idea of turning one to ash...Hollywood."

"A link to the past," Jia Li said, "but to stories, and facts, long forgotten."

"You remember," Jack said.

"How old do you think I am?" she asked. When he hesitated, she said, "Go on, guess. I won't be offended if you guess high."

Jack tried to recall their previous conversations. She'd said something, hinted... "One thousand."

Jia Li shook her head. "Older."

"Two thousand."

"Keep going."

"Three."

"Almost there," Jia Li said.

"Do you really count the years?" Jack asked. "Doesn't it get tiresome after a while?"

"One of the Ramses sent a mission east," she said. "They brought treasures and scrolls, knowledge, and weapons. They meant, eventually, to conqueror. We never let them return. But they brought something they hadn't realized. A vampire, as you call me now, but quite different than the ones in our legends." She pushed Jack away, strode toward the office door, and paused with her back to him. "No, I do not count the years, not exactly. I cannot. Our years were different than yours. Calendars have changed and shifted. Time, my love, is a matter of perception, nothing more. I'm twenty-nine, according to most who guess, and that works fine for me. As to your doppelganger friend here, you were right. His appearance would normally lead to your death. But he'd be the one to kill you."

"How do you know about doppelgangers?" Jack asked, not letting Jia Li leave. "They're not exactly related to vampires. Or China."

"I've been around."

"Tell me," Jack said.

She tilted her head and narrowed her eyes.

"Tell me," Jack said again. "I mean, that's what I do, I collect stories, right?"

Her smile widened. "What's your angle?"

"No angle," Jack said. "I'm just...interested."

"I met one once," Jia Li said. "She looked just like me. Five, six hundred years ago, I don't remember. But she hadn't always looked like me. I saw her shifting from someone else. My eyes were quicker than her transformation. They're parasites. They need someone's shape to assume, but they don't like to be seen. Can't stand light, either. This one, he might have run away, but he would have come back to kill you."

While she spoke, she'd walked casually toward Jack. She sat on the edge of the desk, legs crossed at the thigh and hands on her knees. "That good enough for you?"

"You could have told it better," Jack said.

"More action? Philosophizing, perhaps? Moralizing?" She laughed. "Okay, the moral of this story is, don't trust what you see in the mirror."

"That's a little trite."

She slapped his cheek. It stung. He nearly fell off the chair. "You asked for the story." She bent forward, gently taking his face in one hand. "Anything else you want?"

Jack met her eyes, felt himself sliding into them. Still, he managed to say, "No."

She scowled. "It'll be night soon," she said. "I imagine we should expect visitors."

"You sound like we're a couple."

She smiled. "We *are* lovers." She kissed him, hard. Unnatural bliss, like gauze, veiled Jack's senses. But Jia Li pulled abruptly away, jaw hanging open, staring out the window behind Jack. He managed to turn.

The rain no longer fell. It floated there, in the form of a face with eyes as large as Jack's head. It grinned, then smashed the window.

3.

Jack knew names without knowing how. He would have recognized Jia Li as a vampire on sight even if she hadn't been drinking. He'd recognized the homeless man as an errant zombie, the wraith for what it was. Sometimes, it wasn't immediate. Sometimes, the names meant nothing to him.

The face in the rain was no shadow or phantom; it was the water itself, an *elemental*. Jack knew nothing about it.

When the window shattered, he fell out of his chair and rolled into the bare wall. By the time he looked again, the elemental had assumed a human-sized shape to step into the office.

Jia Li crouched in a fighting stance, low and back, one leg forward, hands open — like blades.

"He's mine," she growled.

The elemental ignored her. Wind and rain poured through the open window, spraying Jack, adding bulk to the elemental. It stepped toward him.

Jia Li attacked. She leapt, kicking with her back leg, striking the elemental's head. Her foot splashed through it without resistance, splashing water everywhere. She landed beside the elemental and smashed its chest with both palms.

Jack had no doubt that, had she kicked his head, it would have come off. Those palms would have shattered ribs.

The elemental lost its form and cascaded like a sudden waterfall, drenching Jia Li.

Jack leaned heavily on the wall for support as he stood. The elemental reformed behind Jia Li.

Before she could react, it enveloped her. However she moved, it mimicked exactly, as if a part of her skin. She ducked, then rolled across the desk trying to shake it off. The water clung to her, flowing around her, following every move. She opened her mouth but got only a deep breath of water.

She spit it out. The water erupting from her mouth fell back, a horizontal fountain, crashing into her face and neck.

She slammed backwards into the outer wall of the office so hard, it shook. They left a damp silhouette. She looked briefly at Jack, then flung herself out the window.

Jack staggered to the desk to watch Jia Li's descent. She crashed onto the roof of a nearby building, landing poorly and rolling aside. Water exploded around her. Reforming into the shape of a man, it looked up at Jack. Jia Li lifted her head and bared her teeth — or maybe Jack imagined that. They were too far to see detail through the storm's shifting shadows.

He didn't stay to watch. He reached the office door without falling and leaned on the wall in the hallway. He found the elevator. Briefly, he wondered if it was safe; but he was too high up, and too weak, to risk the stairs. He punched the button and waited. Wind rushed through the shattered window and raced down the hall, bringing a spray of mist.

With a soft, high-pitched ding, the elevator doors opened. Jack fell in. He pushed the Lobby button — and kept pushing it until the doors finally closed and he started to descend.

4.

From the street, Nick saw the window shatter. And it was there, that office building, that the wind and rain pummeled. The storm focused all its fury on one spot: the watcher. Jack Harlow.

He was still more than a block away when the vampire leapt from the building. They were thirty, maybe forty stories up. She cleared the street, landing on top of another building.

A moment of decision: get Jack, possibly still alive in that building, or chase the vampire. If Jack lived, something stronger had tossed the vampire out that window.

Nick crossed the street as he ran and drew his gun. There was no way in hell he would fail both of them.

CHAPTER NINETEEN

1.

The doors slid open and Jack spilled into the lobby. There'd been no stops, and no one waited at the bottom. He staggering, but remained upright.

He didn't have much time. The elemental was still out there — Jia Li was still out there — not to mention the dozens of other things he might or might not have seen.

Immediately beyond the elevators, facing two sets of double glass doors out to the street, was a security desk. The uniformed guard looked up from his panels. "You're wet."

"Window broke," Jack said, not stopping. There wasn't time to make up a story.

"Where?"

"Upstairs," Jack said. He pushed out the door. The rain wasn't going to get him wetter. Wide concrete steps led down to the street. A railing bisected the stairs; Jack held it as he descended.

"Wait." The security guard came out behind him. Jack almost stumbled. "I don't know you."

"Just visiting."

"Then you didn't sign in."

"I don't have time for this."

"I'll have to ask you to make time," the guard said.

"Or?"

"Or..." The guard hesitated, glancing down the street. He was being pummeled by the rain, but someone — or something — had diverted his attention.

Nick bounded up the stairs, gun aimed at the guard.

"Don't," Jack said, holding out his hands as if that might actually stop the hunter. The guard had no weapon; he was probably an hourly employee and minimally trained. He was not part of the night.

"Get back inside," Nick said, pausing on the steps. "Pretend this never happened."

The guard lifted his hands in surrender. "Right. Yeah. Of course. This never happened. I...er...should I call someone to fix that window?"

Jack glanced upwards again. The rain fell straight on him. "Tomorrow."

The guard hesitated, then ran back inside.

"We better get out of here," Nick said, coming to Jack's side. "You look like shit."

"Feel it, too," Jack said.

Nick propped Jack with an arm around his waist and helped him down the steps. They walked as fast as Jack could, reaching the first alley before police showed up. They had minutes, at best, to get out of sight.

"Have to get you out of the rain," Nick said. "Someplace safe."

Jack shook his head. "There is no such place." The alley led to a two-lane side street. "Lisa's apartment."

Nick shook his head. "There's a church just down the block."

"Church?"

"Isn't it some sort of sanctuary?" Nick asked.

"You've watched too many movies."

"It's warm and dry," Nick said, "and close. That's most important right now."

2.

Nick Hunter broke a lock to get into the church. It was huge and shrouded in darkness. After an outer hallway, another set of equally large doors led into the nave. Holy water fonts flanked the inside of the doors. Rows and rows of cherry wood or mahogany pews were divided by a wide aisle. Except for a brilliant white Bible, the altar was bare. Huge organ pipes rose on either side of the altar. Stained glass windows depicted the stations of the cross. Rain echoed on the ceiling, simultaneously booming and distant.

Nick dropped Jack into the last pew. "There's no knowledgeable priest to suddenly come to our aid?"

Jack shook his head.

Nick sighed, tucking his gun away. "What happened up there?"

Jack laid back, closing his eyes. "You don't want to know."

After a moment, Nick asked, "Is she dead?"

"Jia Li?"

Nick paused. "The vampire has a *name*?"

"I don't know if she's dead."

Nick didn't think Jack was lying. He wanted to press for answers — partly because he didn't want to admit he'd lost Lisa. "I saw her go out the window."

"She wasn't alone."

"And we won't be for long, will we?" Nick asked. "The sun's low. May as well be night out there."

Their voices carried in the church, but there was no one to listen. A few prayer candles burned in the front and rear corners. The lighting was low, as only a few guide lights in the floor alongside the pews glowed dimly.

"How'd you find me?" Jack asked.

"Followed the wind."

"Ah." A moment of silence. "What took so long?"

Nick didn't answer. He walked toward the rear doors of the church and the silver dishes of holy water besides them. "Quiet in here," he said. "Are you sure we're not safe?"

"Have you never seen a vampire in a church?" Jack asked.

Nick thought about it. He'd seen them in church graveyards. Of course, this was the first time he'd been inside one in over a decade. "No."

"Neither have I," Jack said. "Does that mean the stories are true?"

Nick didn't ask about God. Didn't dare, out of fear of being struck down. There was enough lightning already. The church housed a different shade of shadows. He felt uncomfortable. "Maybe we should keep moving."

"Does it matter?" Jack asked. "They'll keep coming, won't they? I mean, they're following me, and not by any means we know."

Nick looked at his watch. "Dawn is a long ways away."

"Dawn," Jack said, "won't protect me."

"Do you think I can?"

"I'm not asking you to try," Jack said, sitting up. "I'm not really sure why you stuck around. You wanted the information in my computer, right?" Nick didn't answer. "You could've taken that already, gone five hundred miles by now. But you're still here, and you were looking for me."

"I wanted the vampire," Nick said.

"Then go get her," Jack said. "That fall didn't kill her."

"I'm involved now," Nick said. "I can't just leave the two of you to your fates."

"Where's Lisa?"

Nick skipped the question. "If the vampire's still alive, she'll come looking for you."

"Where's Lisa?" Jack asked again.

Nick took a breath.

"She's not at her apartment, is she?" Jack asked, standing and walking; Nick kept his gaze on the doors, away from Jack. The sudden anxiety was exhausting. "Is she dead?"

"She's not dead," Nick said, bowing his head. "At least, not when I last saw her."

Jack grabbed his shoulder. "Tell me."

Reluctantly, Nick did.

3.

"Look at them run," the demon said to Lisa Sparrow, referring to all the scampering creatures. Every turn of his head sent another slew of malformed beasts running frantically for cover, crawling over each other, pushing others back so they could get further away. "They're pathetic," the demon said. "Why don't you run?"

Lisa waited for the demon to continue, but realized he actually expected an answer. "No point."

"No?"

"If you want me," Lisa said, "it doesn't really matter how far or fast I run, does it?"

The demon laughed. "No. No, it doesn't at all. Quite perceptive. Yet these fractured minds around me, they tremble with fear. Fight to hide behind their brothers. Does that seem honorable?"

Lisa tried to avert her eyes. The demon was a solid mass of blister red muscle twice her size, but she couldn't force herself to look at the souls in the molten river, or the deformed mega-insects clinging to the backs of the wretched beasts cowering behind every available rock. Again, the demon was waiting for an answer. "No," she finally said.

"No," the demon agreed. "There is a distinct lack of honor around us, wouldn't you say?"

"Sure."

"And fear," the demon said. "Everyone here, big or small, is frightened. *Of me*. Even you, isn't that right?"

Lisa nodded.

"Yet I have done nothing to you," the demon said. "I have laid no hand on you, nor issued any threat. It's you, in fact, who have done wrong by me, yet you tremble."

"You took me. Kidnapped me."

The demon laughed. "I've done nothing of the sort. *You* came trespassing, without invitation, via a portal you opened by rather illicit methods." He paused, raising a hand as if to stop her from speaking. "Yes, I know, I left something behind, a mistake in the heat of a very unusual moment." He shook his head. "You do not even realize what you've done, do you? This is new to you."

Lisa nodded. It was easier than talking.

"Allow me to enlighten you regarding the full breadth of your actions and all their implications. You unlocked a door that should not have been opened, a door to my world. My *prison*. Five hundred million creatures exist here. Great and small, human and beast, hybrids the likes of which you are simply incapable of comprehending. It's a very big prison, but not the biggest."

"I saw you on the street," Lisa said. "You were already out of your prison."

The demon laughed again. "*My* prison? Look around you. Every soul you see, every beast, they are tortured and disfigured, crying in agony and fear, screaming. Do I scream or cry? Am I...altered?"

Hesitantly, Lisa said, "I don't know."

"No," the demon repeated. "I am no prisoner here. I am the warden. These things around you, they are my charges. And you, regardless of your intentions, have released one."

"I didn't..."

"You did," the demon said. "It's not a question of what you meant or wished for, but what we are going to do about it."

"You attacked us."

"I was deceived," the demon said. "I see it now, but there, in his presence — that no longer matters."

"It matters to me."

"My attack was unsuccessful," the demon said.

"Your vampire girl..."

"*My vamp...*" The demon paused. "I fashioned the golem, and I *influenced* a few weak-willed and easily manipulated creatures. But that vampire — was not under my direction."

"Why attack us at all?" Lisa asked. "What were you led to believe that was so wrong?"

The demon shook his head. "There are more important matters at hand. One of my charges has *escaped*. To your earth. He must be brought back."

"What about Jack?" Lisa asked.

"Your friend," the demon said, "is probably dead. Will you stand by as the rest of your world joined him?"

Lisa barely heard the question. "Dead?" He couldn't be dead; she'd only just discovered him.

"Do you hear me?" the demon asked, closing the short gap between them and looking directly down at her.

Lisa met its eyes, fighting the urge to run. As she'd said, where would she go?

"You must take me back to your world," the demon said, "and let me recapture my ward. You stole my key."

Lisa blinked through her tears. "What key?"

4.

After Nick finished, Jack Harlow sat down again. It was a lot to hear. "So," Jack said, "why are you still alive?"

"I'm sorry?"

"Why didn't the demon kill you while you were there?" Jack asked. "It sent you back."

"I...I don't know," Nick said.

"He wanted something," Jack said. "Maybe it needs Lisa alive." There were possibilities that drove ice picks into the marrow of his bones.

Nick narrowed his eyes. "I can follow a vampire's trail because it leaves one. I can figure which direction is most probable, follow sounds and odors. We all leave trails when we go, unless we know well enough to erase them. But this demon...I don't think he's here."

"Demons can be summoned," Jack said.

"Do you know how to do that?"

"No."

Through the stained glass, a particularly violent display of lightning cast uneasy — and unstable — red and blue lights around them. Thunder echoed under the high ceiling. Shadows, even in the church, bristled as if alive.

"We should keep moving," Jack said.

CHAPTER TWENTY

1.

The demon took Lisa's hand. Until that moment, she'd been unaware of a number of things: the heat had dried the rain completely but now soaked her in a thin layer of sweat; the demon was exactly her height, and proportions in this place shifted; her heart had calmed to its normal beat; and she wasn't afraid anymore.

"When I come and go," the demon said, "I move via a key — or something like a key. It's insubstantial and unremarkable and intangible, but without one I cannot travel."

"You were on earth," Lisa said.

"I was summoned, yes. Granted a weak, impermanent key." They walked alongside the lava river, like friends at a lake with a fountain instead of agonized souls clamoring for escape. "Stupid people play with books and spells they know nothing about. This realm is filled with them." He stopped, bent over the river, and reached in. Everything scattered, but he plucked one soul by the nape of his neck and displayed him to Lisa. "This man summoned me most recently. He has been here, now, five hundred years."

"What about last night?" Lisa asked.

"Time, in your world," the demon said, "flows differently."

The demon dropped the soul into the river. Its scream sounded muted, as did all sounds but the demon's words. "He didn't know what he was doing. He hadn't fully brought me into your world. I had to return. But, I was drawn elsewhere, to your city, by an unnatural urgency. I couldn't resist. I fashioned and enslaving my little army. I separated the three of you, kept you fighting your own battles, so I might answer this unusual need and destroy the watcher."

"*Jack.*"

The demon went on without pause. "When that vampire bitch snatched him, I knew my task was done and came home. The key dissolved, or so I thought." He nodded toward the molten river. "It's one reason they are punished so severely."

"He might not be dead," Lisa said.

"Vampires feed until sated," the demon said, "and leave only corpses."

Lisa clenched her eyes closed. "However," the demon added, "he may have slipped away if something else, equally as compelled, fought to take him from the vampire to kill themselves."

Lisa laughed. It was soft and quick and sounded all wrong here. "What a strange thing to hope for."

"Through all the millennia I have held my post, there have been precisely four escapes." The demon smiled. "Fewer than my predecessor. The most recent, however, when you caught the remnants of that key, was facilitated by you."

"How?"

"I need him back," the demon said.

"I didn't do anything."

"His name is Kaz'azeal," the demon said. "He was never human, not from any realm you'd know." The demon stopped walking, turned to look directly at Lisa. "I am not happy."

Lisa met the demon's gaze. "Neither am I."

"Then you will help me," the demon said.

"I don't know how."

"I will tell you," the demon said. "But first, to show just how important this is — you are familiar with the Black Plague?"

Lisa nodded.

"The Red Death acts similarly, but worse," the demon said, pulling a soul from the river. "Its initial symptoms are like your flu. I contracted it once myself, and for that I made Kaz'azeal suffer greatly. He is a carrier." As he spoke, the soul's flesh withered and came away in flakes. The eyes liquefied. The bones became visible and the skull crackled like a windshield. "He will spread this to your world, and will slaughter thousands regardless. He consumes flesh, human and other. His saliva carries the disease, and his breath. He will grow quickly to his original size."

After a moment, during which the demon reverted to Lisa's size, she asked, "What do I need to do?"

2.

The watcher and hunter walked alongside the lake, away from the streets and most human eyes. Jack felt uncomfortable with the attention. He didn't know how to undo it. But his primary concern was Lisa. With his mind fully his own again (Jia Li had screwed it up pretty badly, albeit by nature rather than malevolence), he realized how much Lisa had given him. The hope of a regular life. Without that — without love — he would have lost his soul to Jia Li. Love gave Jack strength. Inexplicable and sudden as it had been, it gave Jack strength enough to continue walking, despite exhaustion and pain, despite the swirling storm. Into the very depths of Hell, if he must; Jack would go anywhere and do anything to keep Lisa safe.

Nick said little as they walked. He watched the trees, and for shadows that followed. Only the wind, thus far.

Jack glanced across the lake, past the fountain (spewing water despite the onslaught coming down), at a gazebo on its edge. During the day, it hosted weddings and groups of schoolchildren. Now, it was too dark to see if that figure there was male or female, or even human, but it watched them.

3.

Nick saw it immediately, caught it in his periphery: a greenish shape surging like a ship on the water. Straight and tall at first, it was a mass of tentacles, whipping and flailing, twenty yards from shore and getting closer.

Nick drew his gun and fired. He let loose three, four shots, hitting the mark every time. The squid-like thing dropped forward with a splash.

After a moment's silence, it erupted from the water right at the lake's edge. It had come from forgotten times and depths. Nick fired again, aiming for the stalks on its apparent head, those blinking and swiveling things that might be eyes. It lashed out, its tentacles plenty long enough to reach them on the paved path. Nick barely avoiding one; another struck Jack below the shoulder.

A tentacle wrapped around Nick's ankle. It yanked, pulling Nick's leg out from under him. He went down and lost his gun. He scrambled to grab something, but the path was too smooth. The thing dragged him toward it.

Nick bent his knees and pulled himself into a sitting position. He was on the grass now, a patch five yards wide, and being dragged too quickly. He took a stake from his jacket and slammed it into the tentacle just under his ankle.

The thing shrieked.

He shoved the stake down far enough to lodge into the ground. It was moist and muddy, but the spike stuck.

Nick freed his foot and rolled sideways, avoiding an expected attack that never came. He threw himself away from the squid, over and beyond the paved path, and out of its reach — assuming the thing couldn't leave the water.

It came out of the water.

It was segmented, like a giant insect, with tentacles protruding from all sides, eyelet things on stalks emerging from its head, and similar appendages like feet on its bottom third.

Three tentacles bore down on him. Nick rolled backwards, sliding into his gun and kicking it further away. He felt the wind when one limb missed him; it struck the path and cracked the pavement.

Nick glanced at Jack. The watcher was on his feet, retreating. The squid-thing pursued him. Nick retrieved his gun, which was useless, and glanced at his stake. Somehow, despite the water-saturated grass, it had grabbed onto something. The squid went only as far as the spike allowed, then pulled and strained against it, whipping tentacles at a fleeing Jack.

Nick reached for his long knife, but Lisa still had it. Cursing, he went instead for the butterfly knife. It was short, silver like all his weapons, kept at his ankle. If the stake could hurt the squid, the blade — even a mere four inches of silver — would cut it.

He flipped it open and ran.

He didn't attack the beast; that was suicide. He raced around its apparent reach, through the trees lining the outside of the path. The squid thrashed, smacking everything it could reach, and would soon wrench itself free.

When one of those tentacles came near him, Nick slashed with the knife. It cut easily; there was no bone. He didn't sever the end of the limb, but gashed it good. Blood — or something like it — spurted from the wound.

After just one slash, the squid aimed all its appendages at Nick, striking and slashing furiously. Nick stayed out of range, slashing when something came close enough.

Nick pulled another stake.

Years of fighting vampires had honed his nerve. At exactly the right moment, Nick stepped forward and swung the stake. He caught the tip of a flailing appendage and lodged the end of the stake into the tree next to him.

Then he ducked and rolled backwards, out of the way, as other appendages — there must have been thirty — smashed the ground and tree.

The oak was thick and sturdy. Though it shuddered with every strike, it seemed unlikely to break right away.

Two limbs down, thirty to go? No way. Nick flipped his butterfly knife shut and ran after Jack.

4.

Jack had managed to run maybe twenty yards before stumbling. He felt like an idiot character in a bad horror movie; he'd look up to see the bad guy looming, chainsaw overhead, and that would be the end of Jack.

He looked. Nick (not the bad guy), holding his gun (not a chainsaw), stooped to help Jack to his feet. "What is that?"

"Eld..." Jack shook his head, not really wanting to know. "I'm not sure. What happened?"

"Pinned it," Nick said. "It won't hold."

They ran, as best as Jack could, toward Lisa's apartment. They were still a good distance away. While the rain lightened, the night darkened, and quite suddenly there were frogs everywhere. They hopped from the trees and off the grass. Dozens, at first, then hundreds, until they lined the paths ahead of them and behind.

Most were regular tree frogs, mottled brown, no bigger than a fist. Some, however, were bright green, spotted with reds or yellows, sporting huge bulbous eyes; some were as large as a man's head.

They croaked loudly, without rhythm, as their numbers increased.

Jack stopped running first; Nick slowed after only one more step. "They're all around," he said.

But they weren't. They'd left a clear path away from Lake Eola and toward the street hidden by trees and shrubbery. Tentatively, Jack stepped in that direction.

Behind him, the frogs closed in. They seemed like one massive creature, their individual movements no longer discernable.

Nick followed closely. Every step, the frogs closed ranks behind them, leaving the path ahead open.

Further down the path they'd been on, in the dim light under a streetlamp, a man adjusted his hat and took a drag off a cigarette. His trench coat flapped in the wind. He dropped the cigarette and crushed it under his heel. Never once did his eyes stray from Jack. If not for the frogs, they would have run right into a dark faerie.

Jack Harlow had seen a dark faerie just a few months ago, in the low lighting of a bar. He might have been the same one: tall and thin, hiding in the shadows, taking long breaths from a pungent brown cigarette. A woman had approached him, captivated by his glamour. That was how they drew their victims. They had no need for blood or flesh or sacrifice; they killed for the thrill.

This dark faerie, however, did not seem content to watch his intended target walk away.

Nick said, "We have company."

The dark faerie approached the edge of the frogs, who croaked and hopped in growing agitation. He crouched, then leaped.

Nick turned to shoot, but never got off a shot before the faerie landed directly in front of them, squashing frogs beneath its feet, and twisted the gun out of Nick's hands.

His coat spread out behind him like wings. Feline eyes glowed. He bared jagged teeth, hissed, and grabbed Jack by the neck with his free hand.

Jack pulled back, swinging a fist up into the faerie's elbow.

Before Jack or Nick could do anything more, the frogs moved en masse. They leaped on the dark faerie from all directions. Some landed on Jack, but then hopped again. One frog, on the end of Jack's arm, spit in the faerie's eye.

He staggered back, releasing Jack and swiping at frogs. Jack kicked, hard, between the faerie's legs. He crumbled, and the frogs swarmed.

Nick retrieved his gun. "I thought you couldn't fight."

"Not like you can," Jack said.

The dark faerie writhed beneath the amphibian sea as Jack and Nick approached the street.

5.

Nick Hunter looked back twice, to be sure nothing — dark faerie, squid, frog, or *other* — followed them. They reached the street.

"They're coming from far away," Nick said. Not all of those frogs had been indigenous.

"I'd rather not think about it," Jack said.

They were silent for a moment, motionless. A possibility surfaced in the back of Nick's mind, something he hadn't considered before. If all these creatures were attracted to the watcher, regardless of the reason, they wouldn't stop until he was dead. Sure, the beasts focused on Jack, but how many people would get in their way? How many innocents would die?

What if the only way to stop these things was to kill the watcher?

CHAPTER TWENTY-ONE

1.

Nick Hunter, prepared for almost anything imaginable, expected something well beyond his imagining. They took the stairs to Lisa's floor, finding stairwells and hallways unoccupied but her apartment door open.

He led with his gun. He motioned unnecessarily for Jack to be silent. Easing along the wall, Nick peered inside.

The short front hallway led straight to the bedroom; the living room/kitchen area was off to the right. Nick heard a British accent. "Lovely tea, thank you."

He glanced in the bathroom as he moved in. It seemed empty. Jack, right behind him, displayed a decent amount of caution.

Lisa sat on the couch, back to the window. A blond man in a leather jacket sat beside her. They drank tea from ceramic mugs. The pot sat at the center of the glass coffee table.

"About bloody time," the man said, standing. "Jack, be a good chap and close the door."

2.

The rest of the world ceased to exist. In that moment, hope returned to Jack Harlow. Here, alive and well, undamaged by the demon, Lisa hugged him. "I wasn't sure I'd see you again."

"Weren't you..."

She shushed him, kissed him, and kicked her apartment door shut. "Inside. Billy's been wanting to speak with you."

"Billy?" Nick asked.

Jack felt numb. His worse fears had been erased. It didn't matter who else was there. His laptop was on the kitchen counter, the screen facing away.

"So, you're a watcher, eh?" Billy asked.

Lisa led Jack to the couch and had him sit. "He's only been here a few minutes."

"And I only have a few." Billy glanced at the clock on top of the stereo system. "Computer should be just about done uploading."

"*Uploading?*" Jack asked. He was in a state of shock. He was confused.

"To the main database." Billy's grin seemed rather mischievous. "You didn't think you were the only watcher, did you?"

"I hadn't really thought about it."

"*You're* one?" Nick asked. "I never would've guessed."

"You don't listen much, do you?" Billy asked. The laptop beeped. "There, that's about it. All I needed. Good luck, Jack." He placed a flash drive on the countertop. "I shouldn't be getting involved, but I was in the neighborhood. Noticed the...activity."

He walked around Nick, toward the short hall that led out of the apartment. "Thanks, again, for the tea, Ms. Sparrow."

"Wait," Jack said, standing.

"Yes?"

"There are other watchers?" Jack asked.

Billy nodded.

"And there's a main database?"

"Yes, well, you can't access that now," Billy said. "Fix your problem, maybe we'll send someone to talk."

"We?" Jack asked. "What, is it a network?"

"Goodnight, Jack Harlow," Billy said.

"Break a leg, Billy," Lisa said.

"That's theatre, babe. But thanks." Then he was gone.

"That," Nick said, after a moment during which time seemed suspended, "was the most surreal thing I've ever seen."

Jack went to his computer. Whatever files had been uploaded, and to where, he couldn't be certain. He touched the flash drive Billy had left, then looked at Lisa. "What happened?"

She closed her eyes. "It was awful."

"I was there, too, but only for a moment," Nick said. "How'd — how did you get back?"

"The demon sent me back," Lisa said. "I — just got out the tea. I've only been here a few minutes. Billy showed up immediately, knocking, saying he was your friend."

Nick shot Jack an inquisitive look. "Never met him before."

"I didn't tell him about the demon," Lisa said, "or the vampire, or anything. He didn't ask for anything except to see your files."

"It's okay," Jack said. He'd scrolled through a few entries. "Nothing's gone."

"I wonder if there's a network of hunters," Nick said.

Jack inserted the flash drive. "Let's see what he left us."

"There's more to tell," Lisa said. "About the demon. About what I released."

Jack closed his eyes. Arriving at the apartment, finding Lisa — for a moment, he'd been able to trick himself into believing the nightmare was over and the chases were done.

One glance out the window confirmed the truth. The storm might have eased, but the night was neither ended nor empty. Flies gathered outside Lisa's window, spiders crawled in the corners of the room. Watching the watcher. Threatening. Hinting at the greater dangers still waiting.

"Tell me," Jack said.

3.

Lisa told her story, of demons and hellish realms, and the winged Kaz'azeal that threatened to unleash the Red Death. While she spoke, the rain ended. It gave Jack no relief.

"I don't like it," Nick said. "It's lying."

"What for?" Lisa asked.

"It wants you to summon it here," Nick said, "to recapture its prisoner? Sounds a little far-fetched. Maybe he wants to escape himself."

"I don't think so."

"It doesn't make sense," Jack said. "He was already here. Why would he need Lisa?"

"The so-called fucking *key*," Nick said. "If she's got it, if she's it, he needs her."

"What do you think will happen?" Jack asked.

Nick blinked. "I think she'll summon it, it'll kill her and take back this key thing, and then it'll kill you, too. For the same reason it tried to kill you before."

"It could have killed me there," Lisa said, "and taken the key just as easily."

"Maybe it only works in one direction," Nick said.

"You and I both went there," Lisa said. "And back. Both directions."

"We're not demons."

"You're afraid," Lisa said. "You don't know what it is, so you're afraid of it."

"I know exactly what it is," Nick said, looking at Jack. "What's to stop it from punishing you, throwing you into that river? I saw that. *Felt* it. Too damned hot, if you ask me."

Jack tried to ignore their argument, and instead opened the document — the only file — on the flash drive Billy had left.

4.

Imps.
HIGH CAUTION ALERT
Summary.
First recorded sighting: 1123 AD.

Physical characteristics: Tends to move on four limbs, and quickly, though it can walk erect. Sharp claws and teeth of a carnivore. Prefers fresh meat — doesn't need to be human. Unthreatening in appearance. Extraordinarily fast. Climbs well. Regenerative properties — they don't appear to regrow limbs, but can reattach and heal severed fingers. Larger limbs untested. Yellow eyes. Hairless.

Mental characteristics: Mischievous. Single-minded. Love to play pranks, especially with other supernatural entities. Cunning, but not especially intelligent. Basic grasp of simple mathematics and language, but continually devises traps even without potential victims.

Emotional characteristics: Driven by instincts: eat, sleep, procreate. Apparently, its trickster quality is also instinctual. Specimen 183 (Captive) in 1782 AD escaped by faking its own death. Killed all employees (no watchers wounded or directly involved). Specimen 219 (Wild) in 1943 AD killed itself in an elaborate, multi-layered scheme, the exact workings of which remain unknown, that killed three employees and left one deformed (Cross-Reference ROD 353).

Special Note: (Cross-Reference MIL 92 and WAS 219) On two known occasions, watchers have been adversely affected by contact with imps. Case Study MIL 92 was struck by Specimen 138 (Wild) in London, 1523 AD. Blood drawn. Contact caused MIL 92 to lose immunity, and to attract other supernatural entities.

Numerous apparitions sighted. See file (MIL 92) for details. MIL 92 died 18 hours after contact (killed by K'uei Specimen 19 (Wild); see file MIL 92 for details).

WAS 219 was wounded by Specimen 211 (Captive) in 1929 AD. Contact caused WAS 219 to lose immunity, and to attract other supernatural entities. Numerous apparitions sighted. See file (WAS 219) for details. Immunity restored when Specimen 211 was destroyed six hours later.

5.

The file contained nothing else. But it told Jack Harlow everything he needed to know.

He looked up. Nick and Lisa had stopped arguing and were staring out the window.

A skull with yellow eyes under a black hood floated there. The rest of its cloak fluttered in the wind. It tapped on the window with a bony finger, and then beckoned.

"*Ghoul*," Jack said, shutting his computer. "I've seen one before."

"How do we kill it?" Nick asked.

The ghoul tapped the window again, then scratched it, leaving a line in the glass.

Jack shook his head. "We don't," he said, "Run."

CHAPTER TWENTY-TWO

1.

Before any of them were out of the apartment, Jack devised a plan. He paused in the hallway. "Split up."

"What?" Nick said.

"No," Lisa said.

"You're both safer without me," Jack said. "I know what I have to do."

"No," Lisa said again.

He grabbed her, kissed her — too quickly — and said, "Stay here. Hide. When the ghoul is gone, go back inside and stay there."

"But..."

He lowered his voice so only she would hear. "Do what you have to do." He didn't want to leave her in harm's way, but there was no escaping it now. He hoped this would be the lesser evil.

"We don't have time," Nick said.

"You have more weapons, right?" Jack asked.

"Of course."

"Get them. As many as you can. I know what happened."

"What?" Lisa asked.

"The imp," Jack said. "It didn't attack you randomly. It knew I was there, knew I'd try to stop it. It — I don't know how — but it stole my immunity." He reached the stairway and pulled the door open. "We've got to kill it."

"That's it?" Nick asked. "That small little shit that attacked Lisa last night?"

"If you see it, kill it," Jack said. "There's a clearing by I-4, east of the church. One hour?" Nick nodded, and Jack went down the stairs.

2.

Lisa wanted to follow. She didn't want to give him up. He was right, she was safer without him, but she felt less alive. If whatever he intended failed, she'd be left guessing, never knowing for certain. She didn't want to deal with that.

Nick looked at her a moment. "You still have my knife?"

She nodded.

"Keep it," he said. One of the elevators slid open. He held the door. "I think Jack knows what he's talking about."

"You didn't find it yesterday," Lisa said.

"No," Nick agreed, "but I didn't know then what I know now."

"What's that?"

"It didn't go far," Nick said. "If it's anything like everything else out there, it'll be sticking close to Jack."

"That's a good thing?" Lisa asked.

Nick stepped into the elevator. "It narrows the search."

The doors slid shut.

Behind her, glass shattered.

Lisa took a deep breath. No place else to run, she ducked into the maintenance closet. The ghoul shouldn't even bother with her. It wanted Jack.

She held her breath. There wasn't much room: a few shelves, a mop in a bucket, an oversized sink and a drain on the floor, space enough for two standing close. A single, low-watt bulb provided dingy light.

If the ghoul came through her apartment, it made no sound as it entered the hallway. She strained to listen. As far as she knew, it stood on the other side of the closet door.

Under the door, a sliver of light was visible from the overly bright hallway. No shadow crossed it.

She heard the stairway door fall shut.

Lisa drew a deep breath. She clenched her fists until the knuckles turned white. With effort, she put a hand on the doorknob and turned.

The hall was empty. Her apartment was still open. She purposefully ignored the stairwell; the ghoul had probably chased Jack, just as he expected.

Lisa hurried to her apartment.

Shards from one pane of glass were scattered on the couch and floor. The wind wasn't too bad, enough to flutter the end of a magazine on her coffee table.

With a deep breath, uncertain if she was about to make a mistake, she sat in the middle of the room. She ignored the broken glass and the noise from outside, and there was no way in hell she'd look outside to see what else she might find. She knew what was out there: *Kaz'azeal*. She had dreamt of him, or it, and those had been unpleasant dreams.

Closing her eyes, miles from serenity, Lisa recited words the demon had given her.

3.

Nick didn't like it. Sure, separating gave him a chance to rearm. But it also gave Jack a chance to be killed; and Lisa *would* summon that demon.

Damn, damn, damn. When the elevator slid open in the lobby, he didn't know if Jack had made it down yet. He held the doors open a minute or two. Hearing nothing, he stepped into the lobby. Nothing to be seen, either.

He strode calmly through the vestibule and onto the sidewalk. Though the rain had stopped, it left puddles big enough to be ponds.

He intended to avoid the lake.

Nick walked casually down Central, as he might on any other rainy night. Anyone else might be headed to a bar downtown, or a restaurant — for a date, even, if they didn't see him too closely — or to his car parked around the block.

In fact, his truck was maybe two miles away, north of downtown.

This was probably his last opportunity to simply walk away. Whatever hell Lisa unleashed by calling the demon, he was under no obligation to face it. And the watcher — Jack had never asked for his help. Why did Nick insist on giving it?

Because Nick Hunter was stupid. No other explanation sufficed.

4.

Hope.

Such a simple thing. Maybe it was the information on the flash drive, the possibility of a solution, the explanation of the change — and proof *love* had altered his fate. That little bit of information meant Jack Harlow *could* reclaim his life.

But seeing Lisa alive and well, breathing, sitting in her own apartment — more than anything else, that gave Jack hope. A reason to live. He could have a life he'd never imagined, empowered and supported by Lisa Sparrow. There'd be a home, a place to call his own, and someone to share it. He'd never considered these things before. Now, the future burst wide open. Anything, absolutely *anything*, could be achieved — provided he survived the night, found the imp, and killed it. Just that one little tiny thing.

Hope. Jack never imagined how powerful it could be. It gave him strength when he thought he had none. He'd taken the stairs three and four at a time and reached the ground level before the door above fell shut. The ghoul pursued him.

He ran out of the apartment building, nearly knocking someone over on the sidewalk. As far as Jack could tell, he had only one chance. If the children of the night were so drawn to him, he had to pull them in closer — all of them — anything and everything that might be out there. If ghouls, wraiths, vampires, and zombies felt the pull, then certainly that damned imp felt it, and he needed to draw it out.

He ran toward downtown. Not daring to look back, taking no moment to catch his breath, he never slowed. When he reached the red light at Magnolia, he ran alongside traffic and crossed the three lanes as soon as there was a break.

The next block inclined slightly, putting him between the courthouse and a parking garage. He didn't want to guess what demonic creatures lurked there.

At the top of the incline, the road leveled off and headed straight toward downtown. He passed a bookshop, clothing store, tattoo parlor, club, bar, and underground garage. Sushi and pizza, another club, a pair of ATMs outside a bank at the corner. Then Jack reached Orange Avenue.

Orange cut through the heart of downtown. He paused a moment, looking in both directions. South, there was the bar where he'd first met Jia Li; north, her office suite.

Behind him, people walked in and out of the various shops. Some glanced in Jack's direction. Others, heading down the slight hill, might walk straight into the ghoul.

He didn't see it behind him, but that meant nothing. He looked up. The skeletal figure had been floating five stories above the ground when it knocked on Lisa's window. This corner building was one of the tall banks, maybe as high as Jia Li's place. Nothing skimmed down the side of it.

Down one block, almost as far as the ghost's bar, he turned at the corner and ran alongside a familiar parking lot, across the street from the police station, and pulled keys from his pocket.

His Mustang was ahead, the interstate not far beyond it. He intended to lead the night creatures away from the city — then right back to a fully armed and waiting hunter.

Jack thought it was a good plan. But someone waited next to his car.

5.

"Fancy meeting you here." The ash stalker stepped forward. His cane, hitting the asphalt, sounded uniquely loud, drowning out even the rumbling thunder. His black suit glistened in the misty night air. His shaved head nearly glowed.

The mist thickened around them. Darkened. It flowed from all directions.

"No," Jack said — not in fear or awe, not in disbelief, but in defiance. "Won't happen."

The stalker lifted an eyebrow. "Is that so?"

Jack pulled the gold coin out of his pocket. The stalker had given it to him before all this began. "What, do you want this back?"

"I have no need," the stalker said, closing the gap between them.

The mist shrouded the entire street, hiding everything but the two of them. Even the Mustang was invisible. If Jack ran, he might hit a wall, a car, the ghoul...

He rushed forward.

The stalker fell back a step, raising his cane to defend himself — or tap the ground. Jack remembered the blinding flash of darkness before the woman, just informed her life would be long and happy, burnt to ash. There was never a flame.

He wouldn't allow that.

Jack grabbed the cane with both hands and tried to yank it out of the stalker's hands. Briefly, he thought he might succeed.

Then he was on his ass in the street. The stalker towered over Jack, neither laughing nor smiling. He raised the cane.

As the ash stalker lowered it, Jack kicked. He caught the edge of the ebony wood, shifting it just enough so it hit the stalker's shoe instead of the street. A flash of dark followed, and Jack had enough time to wish he'd done something else.

6.

Lisa Sparrow didn't know what to expect, or when, nor even if it would work. She waited, hands on her knees, palms up, in a yoga position. Breathing. Relaxing. Listening.

Wind whistled through the shattered window. The fountain, in the middle of the lake, splashed loudly. An undercurrent of distant engines seemed constant and unending. Sitting, eyes closed, all other senses shut off from the world, her sense of hearing sharpened. She heard spiders crawling in the corners of her apartment, tree limbs swaying in the wind, distant lightning bolts crackling. She heard feet running, a baby crying upstairs, lovers across the hall, oil sizzling on a frying pan, glasses clinking in the wine bar across the street. Hearts beating. A gunshot. Doorbell. A cacophony of music, though she heard each piece distinctly: a local band downtown, someone's tinny radio on NPR, "White Wedding" being snarled out at the arena. She heard everything except her own clothes tearing. That, she felt.

Slowly, Lisa opened her eyes. She saw no demon, no ghoul, no vampire or ghost. No Jack. Just a broken window, its glass everywhere. Clouds churned, ready to release another deluge. Lightning danced across the sky so slowly, Lisa was able to follow it from beginning to end.

She lowered her gaze. Her clothes were torn, her skin bubbling and bulging.

"No," she said, jumping to her feet.

The demon's laughter echoed dimly in her mind.

"No," she said again. The blush of her skin deepened toward the demon's fiery red. "This isn't what we said."

Bones cracked and grew within her. Muscles ripped and thickened. Lisa dropped heavily to her knees. A piece of glass, hanging in the window, fell with the vibration.

She had an amendment for Jack's file on demons: *they lied.*

The demon's voice issuing inside her head: "I knew you'd make an excellent vessel."

Lisa shook her head (the demon's head?) and tried to will her body back to its proper proportions. Chest muscles overlapped her breasts, consuming them. Her legs expanded with a jerk, shattering the coffee table. Eyes burned. Her mouth tasted hot and bitter. One at a time, her teeth popped, lengthening and sharpening, shredding the insides of her mouth.

A wave of agony rippled down over her spine. Lisa hung her head, gripped the floor with crimson fists as blood dribble from her mouth. "You cannot have me."

The demon merely laughed.

Hot needles pricked her brain. Her vertebrae reconfigured, protruding through the stretched flesh on her back.

"You cannot have me," Lisa said again, and raced toward the window.

The demon tried to stop her. One leg almost didn't move, but she demanded it, forced it to push forward. Her body tried to bend at the waist, but she held it straight. An erection burst forth between her legs, merely to distract her. Her whole body twisted, turning over, and she stumbled. She slammed the bottom of the window pane, cracking the wall, scattering more shards. She teetered on the edge, half in and half out.

The demon laughed.

Lisa rocked herself over the edge and out the window.

CHAPTER TWENTY-THREE

1.

When the darkness passed and the mist was gone, the stalker — cane and all — was an ashen statue. Even the individual hairs of his beard had burnt. His mouth was partly opened, an incomplete O of surprise.

Slowly, Jack climbed to his feet. Ashes flaked off, drifting lazily, as if they had all the time in the world, never seeming to reach the street. The wind, which had died within the mist, returned to scatter the ash stalker without a sound.

Jack blinked and inhaled deeply and got into his car.

The Mustang roared to life. Headlights flooded the street. In the rearview, Jack saw the ghoul.

2.

During the fall — to death, presumably — Lisa's life should have passed before her eyes. Instead, she saw flashes of the demon's world: dirt and rock, molten metal and earth, souls crying as they twisted into unnatural shapes. He'd been as much prisoner as warden; he'd used Lisa to escape. His last attempt, done poorly, had been temporary; this would be forever.

His life flashed before her eyes. She didn't understand the importance of any particular scene: a motherly figure bearing a swollen, charred breast; seas of fire; a bridge made of distorted souls that clawed his feet as he crossed. A huge hole, a portal, and the winged Kaz'azeal racing skywards, shattering the unstable opening. Even his second lieutenant cringing at the depth of his failure.

Together, in the demon's body but Lisa's flesh, they smashed the ground.

The apartment building rocked. Concrete cracked beneath Lisa, but she did not die.

When she rose, she was physically the demon, no longer trapped in its own dimension, no longer restricted in its time on earth. And though Lisa's thoughts still directed her actions (the demon's actions), there were desires and thirsts she could not ignore. *Compulsions.*

Blood — not to drink, nor even for bathing, but flowing in her name — the demon's name — and flesh, flayed by her anxious fingers. Above all else, she was drawn west.

The demon laughed inside her head. "You feel it, do you not? The wrongness that must be righted? I can end that suffering. Move aside, give me control, and I shall do all the things I promised."

"And more," Lisa said.

"Much more," the demon agreed. "We shall have a glorious reign!"

"No."

"Allow me to capture Kaz'azeal," the demon said. "Relent, temporarily, and I shall obey the letter of our agreement."

"You've already gone beyond that."

"Have I?"

"I was supposed to summon you," Lisa said, "not *become* you."

"Ah, but if you summoned me, your words would compel me," the demon said, "I will not be commanded like an animal."

"Release me," Lisa said.

"If you had offered another as receptacle," the demon said, "I could have taken the other host."

"You never intended to take anyone else."

The demon laughed. "True enough. But will you stand idle as Kaz'azeal spreads his red death? Can you not hear him now, flying overhead, circling, following the very same instinct that calls us?"

Lisa tensed every muscle, as if that might force the demon loose. Tightened fists, legs, jaw, and eyes.

"It's a burning, inside, is it not?" the demon asked. "Let me quell it."

Her eyes snapped open against her will. "You will give me free reign," the demon said, "or I shall allow Kaz'azeal to spread his disease far and wide."

"What about your disease?"

"I," the demon said, "am beyond disease. I am a nightmare made flesh. You invited me into your body. Give me control."

"No."

She stepped away from the apartment building, beyond the cracked concrete, despite that she tried not to move. "Your will is slipping," the demon said. "You require rest. Sleep. You needn't be bound by those needs. You shall always exist within me."

"This is *me*," Lisa said. "*My* body. *My* soul."

"Not anymore."

Lisa lashed out blindly, an explosion of rage and fury. "Leave!"

The demon laughed. "You are me. I am you. You can no more rid yourself of me than you could excise an unwanted limb."

Another step.

"You cannot stop me," the demon said.

Another.

3.

After ten minutes on the highway, Jack saw nothing in the mirrors except other headlights. He had the speedometer at 70. Police often ignored him, but probably not tonight. He doubted a cop would be well enough armed to stop a ghoul.

Assuming he survived, Jack would change the way he recorded information. *It was 60 degrees with a northwesterly wind, twenty minutes after four on a Friday* wouldn't cut it anymore. That lack of relevant information was what made this sudden turn of events so dangerous. He should know if a simple lock of golden hair could stop a ghoul. Maybe not *golden locks of hair*, but the hunter had learned the usefulness of silver against vampires. Maybe every creature had a potentially simple weakness.

He watched the road ahead of him carefully, half expecting something to be suddenly in his path He checked either side, too.

A biker turned and grinned at him. He was misty, luminescent, matching Jack's speed exactly. The bones beneath his skin were visible, as were white veins.

Jack gripped the steering wheel with both hands. The rider slid closer. With an impossibly thin hand, the phantom knocked on Jack's window.

Jack stepped on the gas. The motorcycle matched him precisely.

Jack swerved to the right lane, away from the phantom rider. The bike mimicked the move, and the phantom knocked again. Harder. Mouthed something, but at 80 mph and with the windows shut, Jack heard nothing.

Jack passed a white van. It carried a metal sliding ladder on its roof, and had the name "Paint by Walter" scrawled in blue on its side. The phantom rider drove through the van, unaffected. Only the phantom's arm was visible, still knocking on his window. The van, meanwhile, swerved suddenly to the left, brakes screeching. The motorcycle burst forward as if nothing had happened.

At the last minute, Jack veered onto an off ramp. He descended a small hill, racing toward a red light. No room to stop. The phantom rider was right behind him.

Jack drove through the light. Horns blared. A car skidded to a stop. Jack turned sharply left, tires screaming and smoking. Overturning, he spun into oncoming traffic under the highway overpass.

Jack turned left again and sped up the on ramp that would lead back toward downtown Orlando — as originally intended.

The phantom rider was right behind him. As Jack merged into traffic, substantially less than 80 miles an hour, the phantom rider took the spot alongside his passenger door. He looked, grinned again, then turned into Jack's lane.

Jack braced for an impact that never happened. The motorcycle, part of it, stuck through his seat and entered his dashboard. Wind still ruffled the rider's pants and jacket. He winked, eyelid passing over the empty socket of his skull. "Howdy!"

Jack shifted lanes, cutting someone off, sped up, switched lanes again. The phantom rider matched every maneuver, never straying from the center of Jack's front seat. "Just wanted to know," the rider said, "if we're headed the same direction."

"Where's that?" Jack asked.

"South," the rider said, "on the highway to hell."

Jack shifted lanes again. The hour was close enough to over. And now, riding back in the direction he'd come, he expected to see the full breadth of his pursuit.

"No," he told the rider.

The phantom grinned and veered left, crossing through a bus and the median, to return to the eastbound lanes.

Up ahead, there was a sudden flurry of brake lights. Jack turned hard to the right, to reach an exit ramp before it was too late; he didn't want to stop, especially considering possible causes of the slowdown.

As he turned, he checked his rearview mirror. Shapes followed him, figures, some amorphous and indistinct. But after

turning, shapes loomed ahead, too — on the sidewalks, in the windows, on rooftops and in the air.

As if fate itself had turned against Jack Harlow, this street was a series of short blocks separated by an endless supply of red lights.

4.

Nick reached his truck without any trouble. He hadn't expected any. He would've smelled a vampire if it came near. But without Jack, nothing would be searching for Nick Hunter.

He reloaded his gun and slipped extra clips into his pants.

He had kept under the seat. In the back of his extended cab, he unlocked a toolbox filled with silver stakes. He slid one into every available hook of his jacket. He kept the butterfly knife, and found the twin of the weapon he'd lent Lisa. He'd felt naked without it.

He'd re-worked the inside of a regular leather jacket to carry a number of inconspicuous weapons.

He wished he had a flame thrower. First thing after this was all over, Nick intended to find one.

5.

Jack drove slowly because he had no choice. He didn't plan to stay on the streets long; he didn't feel safe with the buildings so close. There were too many hiding places, too many holes and alcoves.

On his left, Jia Li's office building loomed.

Eyes were everywhere. It was worse than last night, more densely packed. Dark's denizens had traveled great distances, drawn to Jack. With some luck, he hoped to turn their journeys into sightseeing expeditions.

He tried not to think of the dozens, even hundreds, being slaughtered by things that, if not for Jack, would have been elsewhere. The various beasts and creatures would have done the same on their regular turfs.

He turned at the next street, a few blocks north of where he'd previously parked the Mustang. Almost immediately, space opened up on his left; there was a huge empty lot behind those office buildings. It stretched over the railroad tracks and ended in a copse of trees before the service road and the interstate.

If all of the night closed in on Jack Harlow, they could do so here, in the open, far from any holes for hiding, stalking, or attacking. There'd be no sneaking up on him here.

He checked his watch. He was early and Nick wasn't here. Without weapons, he would not survive. He had only two silver stakes.

Jack parked the Mustang and strode toward the middle of that field. It had been mostly dirt and grass; after the rain, it was now muddy and squishy. The wet ground sucked at his feet.

Something dropped onto his Mustang.

He turned, pulling the stakes out.

Jia Li crouched there, two legs and one hand on the roof, leaning forward, the same position she'd taken on the desk. "Now, is that any way to greet your lover?"

"Fuckin' hell."

She hopped off the car and onto the sidewalk. "You forget," she said. "I'm not here to kill you. Yes, there's this pounding in my heart that says I should, a weight that will lift only after you die." As she advanced, Jack retreated one step to her every two. "You know what I say to that, though, don't you Jack? Fuck it. I've found love."

"You don't love me," Jack said. "You can't love at all. You want blood, sex, nothing more."

She shook her head and sighed. "You don't know what I want or feel," she said. "But tell me, what do *you* feel?"

He narrowed his eyes. "Nothing."

"*I* thought we had something," Jia Li said. "A connection. Physical, at least. You love me, too, don't you?"

"You fucked with my head."

"Not malevolently." She was close enough now to stab. She touched his cheek. "I won't let anything happen to you."

"Step away."

Jack turned. The hunter stood at the edge of the field. He'd pulled his truck into the dirt, and stood next to its open door with his gun aimed across Jack at Jia Li.

"Don't," Jack said.

Nick did not lower his gun.

"Don't," Jack said again. "We'll need all the friends we can."

"She's no friend."

"But I am," Jia Li said, whispering in Jack's ear. "I swear it. I fought for you before. Remember the water elemental. I'll do it again."

"I..." Jack hesitated. He had to say it, though, because it was true (albeit artificial, probably implanted by the vampire herself). "I trust her."

Gun unwavering, Nick slowly approached. "Why?"

"She could've killed me before," Jack said. "She didn't."

"What did she do?"

Jia Li purred, low enough so only Jack would hear.

"She vowed to protect me."

"Why?" Nick asked.

"Love," Jia Li said.

"Love?" Nick asked. "You're a vampire. You have no love."

"Fuck you," she said. "It gets tiresome, constantly hearing what I do and don't feel. You've never been like I am."

"I'd kill myself first," Nick said.

"The hell you would," Jia Li said. "I was as mortal as you, once. The will to live is strong. You'll come back after you die, in one form or another, whether you want to or not. You're the type."

Nick's eyes widened. Jack remained between them.

"You're so strong-willed, so full of zeal for life, you'll refuse death no matter how it comes," Jia Li said, "and you'll certainly never take your own life. Your desire to live is too strong."

"I haven't lived," Nick said, trembling now, "not since *you* destroyed everything I knew and loved."

"You're transparent. You've taken that love and replaced it with a weak need for vengeance. You think, if I can kill just one more, maybe that will even the sides."

"It helps," Nick said.

"It doesn't help anyone," she said. "Look at yourself. Really. You live to hunt. I can smell it on you. You don't even believe in it anymore. You never truly learned to hunt. You pick off the weak like a bully, and you think you enjoy it."

"You're not weak," Nick said, steadying his gun.

"No," Jia Li said. "I'm not."

"I'm still here," Jack reminded them.

A moment passed, and another, in which neither moved; then more long moments stretched until finally, after what felt like hours, Nick lowered his arm.

CHAPTER TWENTY-FOUR

1.

Lisa Sparrow held on to herself in every way she could. The demon pushed and pulled, stretched and crushed. It forced her, one step at a time, toward Lake Eola, in the direction of the compulsion: Jack. It was impossible to ignore.

"I won't let you kill him."

"You cannot stop me," the demon said. "You feel the urge, too. You know its purpose."

"No."

"Give in to it. To me. Eternity will be easier on you if you relax."

"No."

She fought for every ounce of control. She couldn't stop him from moving her legs (*demon* legs, how could those be hers?), so she altered their direction. Pushing one leg too far forward, they fell.

"You're half way there," the demon said. "It can be so much easier."

"Never."

Lisa pushed away from the lake, toward the street, and again she (the demon's body) staggered. "Let me have you!" the demon screamed, a voice only in her mind but full of fury and frustration. She refused. She steeled herself against the thunderous voice, the hellish images of its realm, the external pressure to find and kill.

"Rats. You liked them didn't you?"

She didn't answer.

But through her demon eyes, she saw the rodents. Whiskers twitched. Eyes glowed red. Maybe five, at first, then ten, then twenty — they came from everywhere, the underbrush, the garbage cans behind the building, the sewer gratings.

They swarmed around her, gripping her flesh with their tiny claws and climbing her (demonic) body. She swiped one away. Tried to swipe another, but the demon shifted the direction of her hand.

Rats scaled her back and chest. The first bite was under the ribcage. The second, the back of her shoulder. The nape of her neck. Her thigh.

"I can make them go away."

"They're biting you, too," Lisa said.

"Yes, but I've withstood millennia of torture. How long will you last?"

They bit her arm, her chest— not her breasts, those were gone, but her broad, crimson chest. Tiny sharp teeth ripped and chewed. She stumbled to one knee.

She managed to shake one off her shoulder. Another scampered across her cheek to gnaw on her nose.

Despite her wishes, she was on her feet again, walking — no, *striding*. As she brushed the rats away, the demon controlled their legs.

"You cannot win," the demon said. A scarlet tide surged over her mind, severing her miniscule controls, shattering her thoughts, fragmenting her essence.

The demon grinned, outwardly. The rats ceased biting and perched. He conjured a red glow, a hideous sulfuric smog, around himself. The demon had wrested control of her limbs; whatever spell he cast, she couldn't stop it.

When the smoke cleared, the demon (and Lisa) were at the edge of a field, two hundred yards or more from Jack Harlow, the hunter, and the vampire.

Two hundred yards. She wanted to crawl every inch and tear the watcher — her lover — into pieces too small to recognize. She wanted to consume him, one mouthful at a time, and crush him, smash him, spray him across the night.

"I can expel those desires," the demon whispered, "by fulfilling them."

2.

Ignoring the vampire was difficult. Nick Hunter turned his attention to Jack. "You just want to stand here while the dark unleashes everything at its disposal and see how long you can last?"

"Basically," Jack said.

"You know, that's crazy."

"I know."

"I'm crazy to stay," Nick said.

"Don't," Jack said. "But at least leave me some weapons."

Nick flipped the gun in his hand and handed it to Jack — and also the butterfly knife with its silver blade. Pulling his other gun out of his jacket. "What are we expecting?" He saw nothing, yet, on the field, though shapes and figures were gathering atop the distant roofs.

"We shouldn't have to worry about ghosts," Jack said. "No substance."

Closer, in the wet grass and dirt, Nick saw insects, worms, and rodents. Squirming. Wriggling. Watching.

"Anything else, it's open," Jack said. "After the past couple of days, I know I don't know everything."

"Moon's full tonight," Jia Li said, "even if we can't see it."

"Werewolves?" Nick asked.

Jack nodded. "Possibly."

"What about things we can't kill?" Nick asked. "Like that wraith."

"There are shadows," Jack said, "living mists, that sort of thing. I just have to hope we don't face them first."

"That's not helpful."

"I can handle some of those, lover," Jia Li said.

Nick shivered at the comment.

"The main thing," Jack said, "is the imp. The scrawny thing that was more teeth than face, the creature that attacked Lisa."

"I chased it," Nick reminded him, "but couldn't catch it."

"It's responsible for all this," Jack said. "When it dies, I go back to normal."

"Normal?" Nick asked.

"Untouchable," Jack said. "A DarkWalker again."

"*You* have to kill it?"

"I don't think so."

"And what about the rest of us?" Nick asked.

"What do you mean?"

"You go back to normal," Nick said, "and this whole battlefield — that's what it will be — everything on this battlefield will ignore you. Who do you think they'll go after?"

Jack didn't respond.

"Me," Nick said. "Out of frustration if nothing else." He hoped his ammo would last until they stopped coming — or he could flee. His truck was close, full of gas, easily accessible. But he wouldn't mind fighting until his final breath. Maybe he'd get a chance to take the vampire out before the night was done, but for the moment she might be useful.

"Go," Jack said. "Don't risk your life for me. I've got what I need."

Nick turned, catching movement in his periphery. "Too late."

3.

The man walking toward them stood a little less than six feet tall. Slightly overweight, military cut hair, his skin matched the green of his clothes, with maybe a yellow brown tint and numerous oozing sores. He walked slowly, unconcerned with time or speed. Jack had never seen anything like it, but knew its name. "Bogey."

"Behind you," Jia Li said.

Jack turned, she'd already intercepted a rushing attack. She caught the attacker's arm as it came forward, shifted slightly, and flipped the thing onto its back.

Behind her, Nick shot twice.

"Another zombie," Jack said.

It struggled, reaching for Jack despite the vampire on top of it.

Jia Li slashed its throat with her fingernails. Black juice dribbled from the wound as its head slid back. It continued writhing.

"Sever it," Jack said.

Jia Li pushed her hand through the zombie's throat. Its limbs fell, and she tossed the head aside.

From above, arms grabbed Jack by the shoulders. Two female creatures had swooped down. No taller than their wingspan, three feet at most, they were strong. Their skin had the look and feel of bark. Before Jack could do anything, they'd taken him off the ground.

Jia Li jumped, slashing a wing as she caught a head. She clung to it, swinging downwards as the creature lost height.

Nick shot the other in the back of the head. It screeched, losing hold of Jack, and fled, leaving Jack, Jia Li, and the other to drop.

They landed hard, everyone on top of Jack.

Jia Li ripped the head from its neck and threw it at the retreating creature.

"Harpies," Jack said, pushing himself to his feet. "Watch the sky."

For a brief moment, nothing seemed to move. But Jack knew this wasn't true; in the surrounding rooftops, creatures vied for the best view — night things that did not yet come after him. A shroud had been cast over the battlefield, an unnatural darkness, perhaps to hide them from mortal eyes, perhaps to aid or distract them, perhaps merely to set the stage.

"What if it doesn't come?" Jack wondered aloud. "What if it's content to just watch?"

Nick, seeing the arrivals that were not engaging, came closer. "Do they think it's a show?"

"There's been talk," Jia Li said. "You might not hear it, but it floats on the dark. A watcher who can no longer watch. It's a rare event."

"But they won't attack?" Jack asked.

"I don't attack," Jia Li said. "And neither does your hunter."

Nick glared at her.

"It's a compulsion, an urge," she said. "Have you ever felt an urge that you ignored? Or at least forestalled?"

"Are you saying they're waiting?" Jack asked.

"What I'm saying is, they have free will. As do I. I didn't, don't, and won't kill you, because I choose not to, despite the desire. But it's there, and it's strong, and not everyone — not everything — has the capacity to resist. Or the desire to."

"The imp?" Jack asked.

Jia Li shrugged. "I don't know imps."

"Damn." Jack looked at the buildings in the other direction, where more creatures had taken a temporary perch. "This isn't going to work."

An arm broke out of the ground and grabbed his foot. He tumbled as the mottled hand yanked, trying to drag him into the mud. Another grabbed his wrist. Dead people emerged from the earth.

Nick shot and shot, but out of Jack's line of vision. Jia Li grabbed one of the dead things by rotted hair. She kicked with such power and speed, its head ripped free of the body.

A hand grabbed Jack's other leg; another wrapped around his arm. They pulled him down, into the mud, under the grass. Their grips were like iron.

With Nick's butterfly knife, Jack slashed the decomposing hand that had his other wrist, cutting it deeply. Two more arms wrapped around his waist.

From above, a deafening squawk sounded. A sudden wind rushed over him as something large descended. Jack heard more gunshots, but he was half underground and couldn't see a thing.

4.

"See him struggle," the demon said, "and lose. He's losing. I can make a difference. I can make it a quick and painless death."

Lisa struggled to push the demon backwards, able only to delay it from joining the battle.

"Or I can help him," the demon said. "Save him from the dead beneath the ground, and Kaz'azeal, as well. Do you see him there, the demon escaped from its prison, that thing with the leathery wings and steel claws? It will shred your friends, if the dead haven't already."

Lisa saw all this through the demon's eyes and mind. She knew the full strength of Kaz'azeal — and some of the other creatures out there. She'd run out of options. "Stop the demon first."

"Agreed."

She let go.

The demon rushed forward.

5.

Nick fired again and again, reloading as he moved. He kicked and elbowed his way through the dead things coming up from the earth. He slashed their necks. They went down easy — but there were so many.

He lost his balance in a gust of wind and almost fell. The thing that descended was some sort of demon, twice the size of a man, green-scaled with a long neck and a wicked beak. Eyes like the distended bellies of day-old corpses. It looked like a bird of prey, armored, without feathers — and it dove at Jack, already half submerged in mud.

Damn. He hadn't noticed that. Nick rolled toward Jack, hacking at the dead hands. The limbs he hit fled, but more replaced them.

Nick paused. It was over. Done. The prehistoric bird-like demonic thing was about to reach them; the dead had a solid hold of Jack; Jia Li ripped apart the dead men *almost* as quickly as they rose. And at the edge of the field, a familiar red behemoth rushed forward.

Its steps shook the earth. The dead things stopped. The winged creature squawked again, angrily, and diverted its course.

The demons met halfway, crashing into each other like atomic bombs. Flesh was torn from both creatures and they rolled to the ground.

"Here!" Nick called to the vampire.

Seeing Jack in the ground, she rushed forward. Together, they sliced through the dead holding Jack under.

With the advantage of her speed, and Jack wielding a knife in his own defense, they got him back to his feet. One look from Jack, though, and Nick knew what he was thinking: this was worse than he'd anticipated and it had barely begun.

"Retreat," Nick said.

"To where?" Jia Li asked.

"I can't run," Jack said.

The demons had risen off the ground and crashed back so heavily, the earth seemed to shift its orbit.

One of the dead things grabbed Nick from behind. Jia Li punched it — so close to Nick's head, he felt the wind from her strike. The dead man staggered back. Nick spun and cut its throat.

The dead men were everywhere, some more skeleton than flesh, some held together only by fabrics of rotting cloth. The creatures were three deep, mostly dead, but there were also beasts —the misshapen, hairless, brainless kind of vampire — and things Nick didn't recognize, nightmare things with teeth or muscles or razors.

The sidelines, where others watched, closed in. They were anxious, perhaps smelling blood. They knew an end was coming.

A creature resembling a lion tore through one of the dead men. Its tail was spiked, its teeth in jagged rows, its mane wild and flaming. Nick put three bullets between its eyes before it finally fell.

It was a pointless gesture.

6.

The demon and Kaz'azeal clashed. Lisa tried to ignore the pain as talons ripped through her (the demon's) chest, tore at her legs, clawed at her eyes. The thing was no match for the demon; it made a lot of noise, spilled a lot of blood, but it was definitely the weaker creature.

The demon thrilled at the brawl. He pummeled Kaz'azeal with heavy, thunderous punches that Lisa felt all the way up in the demon's head. It wasn't her body any more. She hadn't become this; it had overshadowed her. She existed beneath, underneath, still alive and breathing. Her own heart beat slowly, steadily, waiting to re-emerge.

"Send it back," she pleaded. "Help Jack!"

If the demon heard her, he did not respond. He tore open Kaz'azeal's chest, and lifted the mortally wounded creature over his head.

"Send it back!" Lisa cried.

The demon grinned. "My pleasure."

The rift opened directly before her. She'd had the metaphorical key; now, the demon had full access to it in her head. A hole opened in the ground, a red sliver of earth beneath a sudden spewing of thick, sulfurous gas.

As the demon slammed the lesser creature down into that hole, Lisa pulled backwards with all her strength. All her will. She needed every cell, every ounce of sweat and blood, every muscle and sinew, every tear, every thought and belief, every wish and hope and dream. She clutched the white bead, the witch's gift, her *bead of light* that was now *inside* her demonic body. She squeezed so hard, the crystal shattered; inside herself, light exploded.

She drew from everything, backwards, taking the demon's legs with her.

For a moment, the demon toppled on the edge of the rift. The red dimmed; the smoke thinned.

Then the demon laughed. "That tickled," he said, though she knew it had done more.

Lisa was within the demon now, whole, an entity onto herself. And she still had the hunter's knife.

The demon's heart had enveloped hers. She had no choice. There was no other way to save Jack. She drove the blade straight through them.

The demon stopped laughing. The demon stopped moving. Cutting with the knife, Lisa tore free of the demon's skin. She struggled loose of the red flesh, which unraveled and plummeted into the closing hole.

Shivering, coated in slime and chunks of demon blood, Lisa fell away from the hole and into the mud.

CHAPTER TWENTY-FIVE

1.

Jack had to get off this field. He hadn't intended to make a final stand. He slashed at anything that came too close. Jia Li and Nick cut down a lot of them; since they were not the target, they were generally ignored.

But Jack was already weary. This had gone on too long. Sure, he had hope, and love, but hope dwindled; the imp wasn't making an appearance.

He saw an opening, a hole. He could run, leaving Nick and Jia Li, but he'd only go right into the dark figures at the edges of the field; the vaudoux was there, as well as other things he recognized — magicians, conjurers, princes, priests — and a few he did not.

A wolf leapt at Jack. He didn't see it until too late, and crumpled under its weight. It was half man, not quite a werewolf but similar, foaming rabidly at the mouth. As they dropped, its claws ripped his skin, its jaw went for his throat, and Jack buried the silver knife in its gullet.

Then he saw Lisa.

She lay on the field, where the demons had been a moment ago; now, a tendril of black smoke dissipating in front of Lisa.

"Nick, get her out of here!" Jack cried.

2.

"Find it, find it," Lisa repeated to herself, using the demon's last strengths while she still had them, while she still drew breath. His powers had plunged with him and would disappear with the last wisp of smoke.

She held the stupidest things back. It took effort, and might have slowed her search, but it slowed the battle. The demon had been powerful, and had controlled a dozen or more of those dead things without Lisa's awareness.

With the demon's fading power amplifying the inherent strength of her dreams, she touched minds dark and icy and abysmal. She flicked through the heads of the vampire, the hunter, her lover. His was warm, attractive, and she easily could have stayed, basking in Jack's love until the demon was completely gone. Things watched her.

The demon's power dwindled fast, her strength with them.

She had to find the imp, the teeth that had attacked her. Her life would never be the same, but Jack's could be saved.

She feared touching a mind that would not let go. Most seemed unaware of her presence. *She* was unaware of her presence, not fully understanding what she was doing or how.

The smoke weakened. Her demonic power waned. She rocked back and forth, hugging her knees to her chest, closing her eyes and concentrating.

The demon was gone.

The acrid stench of its portal vanished.

Lisa opened her eyes. In that final moment, she'd gotten it. But it was Nick, not Jack, who ran toward her.

3.

Nick recognized that Lisa wasn't the same as she'd been. She'd reverted to herself; all traces of the demon in her had been cleansed. She'd fought something he hadn't even imagined. He saw it, there and then, the breadth of what she'd seen and done.

He slowed his run. None of the creatures chased him. They were so focused on the watcher, they never moved to stop him.

"Let's get you home," he said, offering a hand to help her up. Unrecognizable fluids and jellies, black and brown and red, covered her. Some of the blood was hers. Her breathing was ragged and rough. She clutched the blood-soaked knife.

She took his hand and met his eyes. "No."

"What do you mean, no?" Nick asked. "You're shaking."

She shook her head as though it was too late. "I know where the imp is hiding."

4.

A dead man grabbed Jack from behind. Another clung to his legs. He toppled over, twisting to land on one of them rather than his own face.

The putrid stink hurt his nose. Flesh sloughed off the dead men when they splashed into the mud. Keeping hold of the knife, Jack slashed the throat of one and stabbed the other in the leg. He managed to get back to his feet.

Jia Li was remarkable, never slowing, never complaining, hardly saying a word. Her fingernails were as sharp and strong as any knife Nick owned. She glanced at Jack once or twice, smiling or winking. Fierce and relentless, she enjoyed the fight.

He glanced toward Nick — and Lisa, dripping filth.

Distracted, he was struck from behind, thrown forward and off his feet. He tumbled, rolling out of the circle that had formed around him.

By the time he got to his hands and knees, the attacker was lost amid the other creatures. The dead men, at least, had stopped sprouting from the ground. Scanning the pack of mythological beasts, he still did not see the imp.

The creatures turned toward him. Mindlessly. He was a light they followed like moths. Jia Li smashed two of their heads together. Shards of bone crumbled to the ground; their dead eyes remained firmly fixed on Jack.

Jia Li, however, did not seem to see the ghoul. Shrouded in a dark cloak, only its skull visible, it swept across the field. It touched a dead man as it moved, pushing it aside; the corpse dried instantly, then split and fell apart when another creature bumped it.

"Watch out!"

Jia Li spun to find herself directly in the ghoul's path. It reached for her with a bony hand.

She kicked its skull. The bone cracked, but Jia Li fell back as if she'd just hit a brick wall. The ghoul passed over her, headed straight toward Jack.

Nick had given him a gun as well as a knife. Jack pulled it out now, though he had no faith in it, and fired. Twice. Three times. At least one shot put a hole in the ghoul's fractured skull, but it continued undeterred.

Jack ran. There was nothing else to do. How could he destroy a creature he couldn't harm?

He didn't have time to reach the Mustang. The dark surrounded him. The icy touch of the ghoul came closer as he fumbled through ankle-deep mud. He glanced over his shoulder. The ghoul swiped at his face. He ducked, slid, and fell.

He turned over. The ghoul grasped his shoulder. Dryness spread and bore through his flesh to the bone. He tried to pull away, but could not. The skull showed no emotion. The moment, a fraction of a moment, ran as if in slow motion.

He didn't understand how it ended.

The dryness hurt, but the ghoul pulled away. Smoke rose from the glowing sockets of its eyes and between its teeth. Flames danced on its robes. The fire burned bright and fast. The ghoul's skull — nothing else — dropped to the ground.

Nick, behind it, held a Zippo lighter. He grinned. "I want a flame thrower."

"You went after it with that?"

"It worked."

Jack climbed to his feet. "You're crazy."

"They're not paying any attention to me. They want you."

"Where's Lisa?"

"Getting in my truck," Nick said. "She knows where your imp is hiding."

"How?"

"Does that matter?" Nick asked. "It's at her apartment. In the basement."

"Damn."

Jack glanced at the truck. Lisa looked back from the passenger seat and smiled weakly.

"Drive," Jack said. He couldn't reach his Mustang, so he followed Nick to the truck and jumped into the pick-up's bed. From there, he pointed his gun and surveyed the field.

The dead things had swarmed Jia Li (or she had swarmed them). Jack crouched. He fired one shot at an advancing wolf. When Nick pulled the truck into the street, the dark spectators parted to let him pass.

Jia Li could hold her own against whatever remained, but there was a definite shift of focus. Eyes, everywhere, turned away from the field. Things took to the air. Figures swirled. One creature loped after the truck. It was mostly shadow, indistinct, half unreal. Jack missed with his first shot; the second hit its back leg. It yelped, slid, and tumbled.

It was getting up again when the truck turned onto another road.

5.

Beings and entities big, small, and enormous, drifted slowly from the field. Some lingered. Some casually followed the truck. Winged things took to the air, and others simply vanished — with or without smoke. A few came together, spoke briefly and quietly, and decided to get whiskey shots.

From the shadows, not unseen but basically ignored, another watcher watched. He stepped out of those shadows. He approached one who remained, a stranger, something he couldn't quite place. It was ghastly, its shell-like armor rigid and stained, its teeth crooked and splintered. It leaned, but not heavily, on a mahogany cane, and exuded a regal air, as though once upon a time this thing was a prince or a pharaoh. An idea had come to the watcher's head. A thought, possibly a belief, so he wanted to test a theory.

"He's stronger, now," the watcher said, referring of course to Jack Harlow. The stranger with the cane regarded him in silence, but did not leave. "If he survives, he's got something he didn't have before."

The stranger leaned forward and breathed a single word. Infused with a question, with pure but weak curiosity, and a touch of impatience. "Yes?" Deep, the voice nearly rumbled. Unearthly, it vibrated through the watcher's bones.

A long moment passed. The watcher steadied himself. He grinned. He knew what he was doing, or at least believed he knew. He said, "I can balance that strength."

6.

The drive back to the apartment was mercifully short, but it didn't feel that way to Jack Harlow. Shadows slid beneath and through the clouds, across rooftops, and around corners. Others came to windows, eyes aflame. Whatever dark atmosphere had covered the field followed them now. People on the streets looked, but only briefly, puzzled, as if they only thought they saw something.

He'd always felt comfortable in the dark. Safe. He'd grown to accept it. Now, there was Lisa, the possibility of real love — and the dark had turned against him. Certain aspects had stood aside, watching rather than actively participating, but Jack doubted their innocence.

Nick drove onto the sidewalk in front of the apartment building. People across the street, sitting outside the wine bar, stared, and maybe made comments, but didn't really respond.

The steps to Lisa's fifth floor apartment came only as low as ground level, but another staircase around the corner went down. It was a metal door, with a slim window along its side. "Locked," Nick said, but that didn't stop them. Nick picked it as quickly as if he'd had the key.

Concrete steps led to the basement.

7.

The basement was a single room under the entire building. Concrete floors and walls. Three windows lined one wall, all near the ceiling. Free-standing shelves held gardening and janitorial equipment. There were stacks of cardboard boxes. Huge bags of concrete mix. Scattered filing cabinets. Stacked desks. Furniture in piles. A few bare bulbs provided light in pools that barely broke the dark.

A second set of concrete steps led to an outside entrance.

Nick stopped at the bottom of the staircase, gun drawn. "I won't let it out."

Jack nodded. He felt comfortable with this hunter's gun. Jack's previous attempt to hunt hadn't worked. He was free of that now.

Though there were no other rooms, there were plenty of places to hide.

A rat atop one of the shelves stared and twitched its nose.

The imp had climbed walls, too. It could cling to the ceiling. Jack looked up and around, walking slowly.

It was in here, waiting, ready to spring. Jack never lowered his weapon. He listened for the clicking of the imp's claws on concrete. He checked behind a mattress propped against the wall. Under a table. In the shelves of an old, shoddy bookshelf.

A sound to his right, toward the basement's center. And Jack swung the gun. There was a dark spot where one of the lights had burned out or been broken. One step closer, Jack narrowed his eyes. He saw well in the dark, well enough to see shapes and a few details. A lampshade on a table. An open magazine. A chair.

A shadow shifted.

Jack aimed. Almost fired. An inky snake slithered deeper into the dark.

The imp sprung from his left. Together, they crashed into a support beam. The gun slid away as they fell, imp on top. Tiny claws on four limbs — one limp, not fully re-attached. Teeth gnashed. It tore a deep rut down Jack's chest.

Jack kicked it off and scrambled for the gun. By the time he reached it, the imp was gone.

It couldn't be far.

A shape in the shadows. Jack fired. The bullet ripped through a pile of magazines.

The imp ran toward the windows. Jack fired twice, missing both times. The imp ducked behind a couch propped on its end. He shot into the couch. The imp screeched.

Jack shoved a coat rack out of his way, knocking over a pile of boxes. As he came around the side of the couch, the imp dropped from above.

Jack fell, into the couch. It tilted, slamming the wall, and slid out. Jack flipped over the side of it. The imp landed next to him.

Jack pointed and shot again. The imp was pure muscle, despite its small size, and fast. It jumped up, away from the bullet. One more shot, and Jack hit the imp in midair. It flopped and landed with a loud slap. Jack put two bullets in its head. He kept pulling the trigger, but the clip was used up.

He stood a moment and waited.

If anything changed, Jack didn't feel it. He hadn't felt the loss of his immunity, either. He toed the side of the imp; it responded like a rag doll.

8.

"It's dead," Jack said, approaching Nick and Lisa at the stairs.

Lisa rushed forward, kissed him with desperate urgency, then collapsed in his arms. For the first time, Jack saw the self-inflicted knife-wound in her chest. She said, "I waited."

Jack went down to his knees, holding Lisa, rocking her in his arms. "You can't die on me," he said, and kept saying. "I love you. I can't live without you. I want to show you things, give you things. I want to live for you. With you. C'mon, Lisa, don't die on me. *Don't.*" But she'd already been dead, since the field, since the demon had taken her; she'd held on only by force of will. She smiled. She touched his cheek.

Until that moment, Jack had never really known fear. When the were-bat attacked, when he woke in the vampire's office, when creatures came at him from water and sky and earth, Jack had thought he was scared. He truly believed it. He'd trembled and sweat and tensed. But now, as Lisa slipped away, his stomach wrenched and his chest tightened. No pain had ever been so piercing. He couldn't breathe, couldn't think, couldn't see past Lisa's eyes.

9.

Nick helped Jack carry Lisa to her apartment. It was too late to take her to a hospital; the damage was too extensive, too thorough. The hole in her chest showed her ragged heart.

Nick didn't know what else to do. He opened Lisa's door, helped lay her on the bed, and even put a hand on Jack's shoulder as he cried. Nick felt tears in his own eyes. He hadn't shed any since Diane and didn't want to now. He really didn't want to.

But he did.

And then he left.

10.

Calmly as possible, Nick walked away from the elevator and out the front door. He heard sirens. He'd made himself conspicuous, and was heavily armed. He couldn't afford to linger, but he wanted to. He wanted to go back upstairs and share Jack's grief.

But it wasn't like him to express such feelings.

Passing the outside doors, he caught the scent a moment too late: under vanilla and cinnamon, a hint of death. *Vampire.*

He swung his arm, striking if it was close enough. She blocked it.

Nick kicked, and pulled a stake from his jacket, but Jia Li parried the kick and caught his arm before he could attack. "I've been training a lot longer than you."

Nick glared. Anger built up inside. Rage. He wanted to tear her throat out, put a stake through her heart, cut off her head, and burn her corpse.

"I thought I'd tell you," she said, "it worked. The urge is gone. The pull. He's no longer a magnet. Congratulations."

Nick knew.

She smiled, sadly, and pushed Nick back. "You're safe from me, hunter. Tonight, let's keep our truce."

Nick sighed, the anger spilling away. "Tonight."

He looked up the side of the apartment building, though he couldn't see Lisa's window from the front. She might have made a good partner. Jack might become one, someday, but not tonight.

He got into his truck and drove away.

EPILOGUE

1.

Awareness came slowly. First, there were sounds: distant city noises, the fountain in the lake, a radio playing "Dancing With Myself".

Jack lay on the bed, staring at Lisa's body, lost in thoughtlessness. Sunlight streamed in through the window. It was a perfect blue sky. Her body was cold. Stiff. The demonic blood had done horrible things to her insides.

"Please don't cry."

Jack rubbed his eyes. "Lisa?" He smiled, reached toward her. She held up her hand, but they couldn't touch.

"I'm gone."

He clenched his eyes shut. Nodded. "You shouldn't be."

"I am."

His unsteady smile widened. "I'm a *DarkWalker*. We can still be together."

She shook her head. "I can't stay," she said. "I'm going away."

He opened his eyes. The whites were raw.

"I'm going away," she said again. "But I'll always be with you. A little."

"I can't..."

"You can," she said. "You don't have to end like this. My time is over. This...this gift...Jack, I love you. I will always remember you, whatever happens next. And I will miss you."

"I can't," he said again, leaving it at that. He wiped moisture from his eyes.

She touched his chest, the untended wound the imp had left. It was infected and needed medical attention. "I love you," she said again, "and I want you to live. For both of us."

"I'll stay," Jack said. "We can talk about...about anything. We can stay together."

"Only a short while," she said. "I'm — being pulled away. I won't be here for long."

"For as long as we have."

They talked, then, about childhood dreams and carnivals and fairy tales, and other silly things. They laughed. She convinced him to drink water, to eat, to wash himself. And slowly, she faded. Within a day, she was gone.

Jack Harlow lingered a long while before leaving.

2.

The ghost Lisa Sparrow watched from the bedroom where she'd died. She didn't know what was going to happen to her next. She wasn't going anywhere. Tricking Jack's eyes had been easy. Her own heart, however, crumbled to dust when he left. She cried real tears then, drops that left wet dots on the bed.

COMING SOON:

DARKWALKER 2
INFERNO

NOTES AND ACKNOWLEDGMENTS

I wrote the first draft of the first version of this book
so long ago, I barely remember it.

Thanks to everyone at Evileye Books for publishing the
first edition of this book (and Mike Oliveri for the
introduction). Although it's been heavily revised since
then, it was a vital step in the evolution of this series.

Thanks to everyone who read, enjoyed, reviewed,
criticized, or threw *DarkWalker* across a room. This
new edition is leaner, stronger, and in many ways, a
collaboration between me (2018) and me who wrote it
first (2002) and me who revised it previously (2010).

The rest of the series never made it to print.
They are coming.

Special thanks for the continued support of Mery-et
Lescher. None of these happen without you.

Thanks, also, to all my First Readers on all my projects;
the Five Horsemen (Mike, Mikey, Coop, Brian); my
various inspirations; anyone who has ever taught me
anything; the ghost of Edgar Allan Poe; and my Mom.

I have missed people. I always do. I am so sorry.

And as always: Sabine and the Rose Fairy.

ABOUT THE AUTHOR

John Urbancik was born
on a small island in the northeast
United States called Manhattan
at the dawn of a terrible and terrific decade
and grew up primarily on Long Island,
but he has lived in Florida, Virginia, and Australia.

His first novel, *Sins of Blood and Stone*,
came out in 2002.

DarkWalker was originally published
in 2012 as the first of a series.
The rest of the series has remained hidden.
Until now.

John Urbancik also hosts a podcast, InkStains,
based on his writing project of the same name.

www.DarkFluidity.com

www.ingramcontent.com/pod-product-compliance
Lightning Source LLC
Chambersburg PA
CBHW021218250626
47155CB00008B/2864